Published by Lulu for

www.connectionsbooks.co.uk

This edition first published in June 2014.

Paul Stuart asserts his right to be identified as the author of this work under the Copyright, Designs and Patents Act 1988.

ISBN: 978-1-291-90551-9

ALSO BY PAUL STUART

Connections – Who Did You Sit Next To Today? (Paperback)

Connections 2 – Hell Has No Fury. (Paperback).

The Mobile and The Ring – The John Lomax Story (Paperback)

The Mobile and The Ring – The John Lomax Story (Hardcover)

ACKNOWLEDGEMENTS

Once again I must recognise the unflagging encouragement and support of my wife, my mother and father. You are my rock and without you I am nothing.

Thanks must also go to my friends who have been there constantly and encouraged me along the way; especially Carolyn, Debbie, Janet and Geoff.

I must also give thanks to my friends at St.Piran's who have done more than they know, and Rosemary Aitken, who set me on this journey.

Tiffany Truscott at Radio Cornwall....many thanks...there is a part waiting for you!

There are, of course, many others, but it is dangerous to attempt to name them because I'm bound to omit somebody important and that would never do, but they know who they are.

I should also extend my gratitude to all those who have bought my books. I may not know all of you by name, but I hope you continue to do so!

Please use the website blog to let me know what you think.

PROLOGUE

From Connections 2 – Hell Has No Fury

Leanne disconnected the call and turned her attention once more to Billy.

"I'm not going to kill you, Billy. You are my son, and I couldn't do that. But you need to appreciate that I have to send out a message. Just one finger: then a photo with bandages. I'll make sure it's quick." She nodded again and Billy was given a sharp jab in the arm with a syringe. "For the pain," she said. "We'll wait a moment or two to let it work."

Billy cried out, but the hood muffled the sound. That moment or two saved Billy's finger as a dozen armed police with dogs crashed in through the door. Leanne's two accomplices were rapidly pinned to the floor with a barking dog standing beside each. Each man had been bitten and was bleeding heavily from an arm that had been grabbed and held onto by the dogs as they were wrestled to the floor. Leanne was face down on the floor, hands in cuffs behind her back in an instant. Billy was released and, wobbly and groggy, taken carefully to a waiting car. He was not in much pain, despite the dreadful blow he had taken to his hand, because the pain killing injection was now taking effect. He later returned to Australia and settled into life with the girl from the radio station.

Leanne Lane was convicted of abduction, GBH, and, most crucially, being responsible for the murder of DCI Sandy Lane. She was handed a life sentence. She did not have to be held in isolation as she was popular with fellow inmates, having killed a policeman. A few weeks into her sentence, Ray Quinn paid her a prison visit."I won't stay long," he said. I am just delivering a message for John. He asked me to read you this:"Hell has no fury like a woman scorned, but about a wronged man you should be warned."John Lomax had discovered that the only way to keep a secret is to never tell a living soul. It's the only real way to guarantee anything. But it has a price and that price is isolation, loneliness and silence. Isolation is frightening and loneliness is insidious; but silence is different. It encompasses isolation and loneliness. It is not quiet because it has a shattering noise all of its own and it gets into your very being.He screamed his frustration and heartfelt agony. He knew then that he would be lonely for the rest of his life and that he probably deserved it. It was the price he would have to pay for Karen's love turning to hatred and Leanne's love being scorned. He had tested the old quotation at least twice and felt the power of its truth for himself. He fervently hoped that DCI Sandy Lane had felt as lonely and desperate before he had passed on. It felt particularly strange to be so inextricably bonded to his greatest enemy, and to know that there was no escape from that tie for either of them, even in death. In his hands he held the ring that Ray Quinn had retrieved from Leanne before the police had taken her away and a mobile phone. He looked at both and considered the trouble they had caused. He heaved a heavy sigh and hurled them as far as his strength would allow, out from Westminster Bridge and into the murky water of the River Thames.

-1-

The mobile and the ring had hardly caused a splash as they were gobbled up by the river and the dark and murky waters mirrored his mood as he gazed down from the bridge. The current was fast and strong and he felt weak and helpless by comparison. He gazed down into the impenetrable night at those dark and gloomy waters and they mirrored his mood. The river had digested the mobile and the ring as if it were a living thing, without so much as a minor splash and it seemed to him that he might as well leap over the railing and follow them. John Lomax had never felt so alone.

He was totally unaware of anything or anybody around him as he gripped the rail, first with his left hand and then his right. He stood motionless and for him time stood still. The rain soaked his clothes but it didn't matter. His mind was crystal clear as he recalled the glorious hours he had spent making love with Leanne. He remembered the particular things they both enjoyed and the small murmurings of pleasure in his ear. Her perfumed smell was with him and filled his nostrils. He could actually feel her touch upon him as if it were real. They were such precious times, such wonderful moments. His heart broke and tears mingled with the rain upon his face. With an anguished cry he put his left foot on the railing and began to push upwards.

He was lifted up and he felt himself floating, but it wasn't the water that bore him. He became aware that he was airborne and being propelled backwards away from the parapet. His head thumped into something hard when he landed and he lost consciousness for a few seconds. When he opened his eyes his head hurt like hell and he was struggling to breath. He managed to sit up, but felt nauseous.

"Sit still, damn you. Don't struggle. You're safe; I've got you."

John Lomax stared up into the face of Ray Quinn, who just looked straight back at him with unblinking eyes and waited for his friend to recover his senses.

"Well, I guess we're even now," whispered The Biker. "I've got something for you which you need to hear. If you still want to jump after that I won't stop you. Listen and then decide. I'll throw this phone in after you if that's what you want, but at least listen."

John Lomax felt a mobile phone being held close to his right ear and heard the voice of Billy Lane.

"John, I am at a loss. I have lost my Father, but feel no regret. That part of my life will remain a dark and dangerous black hole and I must now seal it up. My Mother, however, is another matter.

Although she is lost to me, she is at least alive and this gives me cause for hope. I don't know how I'll cope without being able to see her. You have been such a rock in my hours of need, so I turn to you. There is nobody else."

Quinn interrupted his reverie. "Now John, what do you want to do? I have to tell you there is more, but we need to get out of this rain and away from here. We don't want to attract any more attention than we already might have. Let's go."

Lomax noticed that his friend had not given him time to answer his question and before he knew it he was being walked firmly off the bridge and into the darker recesses of a dingy London pub. Very soon after that an unnaturally large whisky sat invitingly before him on the sticky wooden table as he began to read.

BILLY'S HOSPITAL RECOLLECTIONS SENT TO JOHN LOMAX FROM AUSTRALIA UPON HIS RETURN. THESE ARE NOT RAMBLINGS; THEY HAVE A POINT.

At the tender age of ten I had to go into hospital in London. In those days children were often parked amongst adults and I ended up in a men's ward. My appendix was removed and so was some of my innocence. At the time we lived quite a way from the hospital, so visits were difficult, especially as I had a younger sister who wasn't allowed in. I remember being torn between thoughts of relief because I wouldn't have to tolerate her constant chatter and homesickness because I loved her and missed being at home. I didn't think it usual to be in such a place for something as mundane as an appendectomy, but I had had a heart problem from birth and thus it was deemed necessary to place me in a specialist hospital on a men's ward.

Not unnaturally my fellow patients all seemed ancient to me and loneliness gripped me very quickly. I felt small and vulnerable. That feeling was certainly not eased when I looked around the ward and took stock.

Directly opposite was a grey haired individual who hawked, hacked and spat his way through my first day. Granted he used a receptacle, but I'd never seen nor heard anything like it in my life. On his left from my viewpoint was a thin bony skeleton which hardly seemed to move. His eyes, which were sunken into his completely bald skull, also never seemed to move. He had a sort of fixed, glazed stare. I did spot him move his arm once, but that was just to pick his nose.

To the right of the hacking man lay a grizzly bear. He was massive and had tubes and pipes appearing from every conceivable orifice and wires strapped everywhere else. I remember he moaned and groaned a lot, but nobody seemed to take any notice, so he just continued anyway. Looking back, I think he gained some relief just by doing that.

Beside me in the bed to my right there resided a most peculiar person. Or so it seemed to me. I couldn't keep looking at him because I was old enough to have learned not to stare for fear of giving offence or causing trouble. However, it is human nature to take in one's surroundings and I wanted to make sure I was safe! He was probably not very old and may have been a perfectly nice man, but he unsettled me by staring back. Surely, I thought, he must know it is rude to stare, but he just kept doing it. His eyes were a piercing blue; he had a mop of jet black hair on his head and much more of the same on his chest. He had no tubes or wires and so could move freely whenever the fancy took him, which it did quite often. I noticed that he visited every patient that I could see from my bed and talked in hushed tones to each. After such a visitation each bedbound recipient would be agitated and call for urgent assistance. Thankfully he never visited me, presumably because he thought it not so much of a challenge to upset a small boy, but I kept an eye on him.

Immediately to my left was a middle aged chatty man. He was quietly spoken, read his newspaper and his book and offered me sweets. I liked him.

The first night was very frightening and I tried not to sleep until I was sure everybody else was asleep first. I reasoned I would be safer that way. The plan didn't work. The hacking man did not sleep at all; he just carried on with his noisy, juicy expectorations and nobody came to check on him. The nurses had no need of a bedside alarm for him because they knew that if he went quiet they should come running. Skeleton Man, to his credit, moved even less at night. I think he was rehearsing for the time when he would close those staring eyes for the last time. However, he woke on my first morning, picked his nose as usual, and just lay there waiting patiently for the day to unfold. Grizzly actually slept all night, although I still don't know how. He snored and roared his way through the night, with his tubes and wires bouncing around and upon him. Again, the nurses paid him no heed, presumably employing the same principal as they did for Hacking Man. Old Blue Eyes was actually strapped to his bed at night. He had obviously made too many visitations and the nurses didn't want to be disturbed. Actually, I realise now that the way each patient was treated at night was individually tailored to ensure the nurses were not needed at all. Very clever, I thought. My chatty, book reading friend to my left was the man who discovered the real reason for this and shared his secret finding with me. He had, he told me before lights out, discovered that the doctors and nurses were playing a real life game of the same name during the wee small hours and made every possible arrangement not to be interrupted. Why my newly found friend should think a ten year old would be enriched by this knowledge I couldn't say, but it had a profound effect for years to come.

My operation took place on the second day of my stay. I don't remember much about it as I was asleep at the time. I was grateful for this because I had not slept at all on that first night. When I eventually awoke, I noticed an empty bed across the ward and asked my chatty friend about it. He looked at me morosely and said that Skeleton Man had picked his nose for the last time and was no more. I didn't respond, but remember thinking that I wouldn't like to be the next person to take up residence in that particular bed.

That's None Of Your Business -Paul Stuart

One incident that amused me happened on my fourth morning. By that time I had been allowed out of bed. Nowadays they boot you out of bed just a few hours after surgery, presumably because they don't want you getting used to the good life of doing nothing, eating their food and making a nuisance of yourself. On that morning the doctor, accompanied by the terrifying Matron, stopped at the hacking man's bed and in a voice loud enough for all to hear declared that cigarettes were the cause of his condition, it was not going to improve and would almost certainly kill him. He went on to advise anybody who was listening, which was everybody in the entire ward, if not the entire hospital, that smoking was sinful and he resented treating patients who ruined their own lives by practising such a filthy habit. Moreover, he railed, he would in future think twice about treating people who damaged themselves in that way. That was quite a radical thing to do in those days, but he has turned out to be quite a forward thinker. Anyway, when he and Matron had swept away in a cloud of disgruntlement, a few of us gathered on the balcony to get some much needed fresh air. The balcony overlooked the street and the front entrance to the hospital. On the opposite side of the road we could see a sweetshop, which obviously also sold newspapers, magazines and cigarettes. We watched with mild disinterest as people came and went, but our attention was caught by our eminent heart surgeon striding into the shop. He reappeared a few minutes later with a paper tucked under his arm and stopped on the pavement. He removed something from his pocket, put it to his mouth and lit it. With obvious satisfaction he drew a deep breath before exhaling a cloud of blue smoke. This drew a round of applause from our balcony and, after looking up at his cheering patients, he scuttled away in deep embarrassment. Skeleton Man would have smiled if he could.

Ironically the surgeon had been correct in his analysis and Hacking Man passed away that night. That meant that two of my fellow inmates had been taken by the grim reaper and it was only my fifth day. This set me thinking and I realised that if the attrition rate continued at the same pace, it wouldn't be long before my number was called. Unfortunately I had been told that I would not be due for release until at least ten days after my operation. I have to admit that I showed signs of panic. After all, I calculated, I therefore had to somehow survive for the best part of another week and there weren't that many patients left on the ward in front of me in the queue. Of course, I was relying on the fact that we would be taken in strict order of admittance, but I couldn't depend on that.

That's None Of Your Business -Paul Stuart

When my mother visited me that afternoon I managed to persuade her that I would be available for release within two days. She was doubtful, but between us we managed to cajole the surgeon and Matron to agree to the plan with the proviso that I could walk properly, that my eating and toiletry habits had been returned to normal and that I would return to have stitches removed on what would have been the tenth day of being an inmate. I was overjoyed, not least because it reduced the chances of my maker catching up with me in hospital. He may have had other plans for me elsewhere, but at least I was giving him a run for his money. My plan was further vindicated when I awoke the next morning to the news that Grizzly had been taken during the night. Apparently, even the plethora of tangled tubes, pipes and wires had not saved him. This worried me greatly because I realised that if all those accoutrements had not been able to save him, then what chance did I have with no attachments to protect me? I never did find out what his problem was.

So, six days and five nights had elapsed and three fellow patients had disappeared. Even my ten year old maths could work out that it was imperative my escape plan worked. When I awoke on my sixth morning I was staggered to learn that all of my previous day's companions were still present and correct. I reasoned that the odds had been tilted back in my favour a little. By this time I was able to walk reasonably well, although the stitches pulled uncomfortably. Toiletry habits were returning to normal, or as normal as possible given the awful hospital food with which we were provided. I had discussed my plan with Chatty Man and he ventured that I was being very sensible because if the law of averages in the ward didn't get you then the food would. He admitted that he had noticed the mortality rate and was very worried because he was next in line.

As it turned out he was wrong. Chatty Man and I had noticed that my neighbour with the blue eyes, who was strapped to his bed each night, had not had his bindings removed that day and was very still indeed. As there were no monitors with tell tale beeps that hover over each patient as is the norm nowadays, nobody could tell whether he had just decided to continue sleeping in order to avoid the perils of breakfast or something more sinister had happened. It was mid morning by the time a diligent nurse took some notice and discovered his unblinking blue eyes gazing up at the ceiling. Curtains were hastily drawn around his bed, which, apart from cutting off my view, was also rather unfriendly, and several other nurses and Matron scuttled into that sanctum. A senior looking doctor appeared and I heard him make an authoritative pronouncement to the assembled crowd. I didn't catch what he actually said, but the meaning was clear from his low rumbling tone. Curtains were then drawn around everybody's beds, which annoyed us all as the developing drama had become the highlight of the day and we wanted to see what happened next. As if by magic, when our curtains were removed, Strapped Down Man had disappeared and a freshly made bed stood there, inviting its next victim with its crisp white sheets, neatly turned down to resemble a toothless maw topped by a perfectly laundered pillowed headstone.

Being only ten years old I didn't know where hospitals put dead bodies, so I imagined another ward which was gradually being filled by my erstwhile companions. I confided to my chatty friend that I thought they wouldn't take much looking after and that at least they were avoiding the hospital food, but he didn't seem to find that funny and returned to his newspaper for quite some time. There wasn't much time for anything else to happen because I was let out the next day. The most long lasting memory of that hospital stay is something that didn't happen, rather than anything that did. My father did not visit once. I still resent it. Mum said he was extremely busy with his police work, but I became increasingly aware of his lack of parental interest and we gradually grew apart. I never forgave him for that, not even when he died. The other memory is that my parents split up during my stay and my father had moved out by the time I arrived home. I have bitter memories about these things."

"John, I have bitter memories about so many things. I have learned much more about dead bodies and people's motivations in life. I know too much about these things and I have nightmares. Help me to at least have better thoughts and peaceful nights. I know Mother and you had some happy times and no doubt some fond memories. Please help me to have some of my own."

-2-

Ray Quinn studied his friend as he read Billy's entreaty. He knew instinctively how much pain Lomax was feeling and did not interrupt. He knew what it was like to be so utterly low, so profoundly without hope. He had experienced it in the aftermath of the London bombings. He remembered how John Lomax had come to his rescue and helped him recover both physically and psychologically. They had been firm and steadfast friends since that dreadful day and he shared his angst.

For his part John Lomax's eyes welled with the tears of loneliness and despair and he turned his head to the wall to hide his weakness. All he wanted at that moment was to sleep and never wake up. It was all too much to bear.

He pictured Billy, totally alone, on the other side of the world. He imagined the horror of his nightmares and the grinding treadmill of his days. He wondered how long Billy would survive without hope; without so much as a sliver of a chance of seeing his mother and living with the knowledge of what a monster his father had been and the ignominy of his death. It was as if Billy had become the son he'd never had. His shoulders slumped as he attempted to wipe his eyes without being seen.

Ray Quinn placed another large whisky on the sticky wooden table and watched his friend closely as he struggled with Billy's demons as well as his own. He allowed Lomax time. He waited for him to fill the space. Eventually Lomax turned his head from the wall, ran his trembling hands through his hair and raised his damp and misty eyes to meet those of The Biker. Quinn saw that they were devoid of light and there was no life behind them. He recognised the unmistakeable plea they carried; the despairing, deep pain. The Thames had taken more than just the mobile and the ring.

He had waited long enough and Lomax had not filled the space.

"John, my friend, we need to do something. I don't mean you; I mean us, both of us. We are not going back to the bridge. I've got you this far and you're not going back. Don't try or I swear I will stop you and you won't like how I do it. Take one step at a time. We'll get you out of those wet clothes and find somewhere to eat. Then we'll sort this mess out."

The Biker had deliberately taken control and Lomax was grateful beyond words.

Quinn phoned his wife while Lomax showered and changed into dry clothes. It was not a long conversation, but she indicated her understanding and agreement. He had completed the call before his friend came back into the room.

"I've got one or two ideas, John. Let's eat and we'll talk."

-3-

Billy's mother, Leanne Lane was serving a life sentence for the murder of her estranged husband DCI Sandy Lane. She was both respected and popular amongst inmates. Her popularity stemmed from the fact that she had got rid of a hated policeman, and their respect was founded upon the knowledge that having killed once she was obviously capable of doing so again. She had never showed any sign of that, but nobody was brave enough to upset her. Leanne, for her part, was content with the state of affairs and her time in prison passed on its slow, inexorable way without many hitches. Her prison guards also showed her similar leniency because they believed she would never repeat her crime. It had been, they reasoned, a "one-off", purely aimed at DCI Sandy Lane whom they knew she hated. From an early stage she had never given them any trouble at all and, because they also all knew Sandy Lane's history and resented the ignominy he had brought to "the authorities," they were content to let routine take its peaceful course. In their eyes justice had been served, albeit of the roughest kind. She was therefore deemed trustworthy enough to spend time in the prison garden and, with the help of other inmates, was making a good job of growing vegetables for the kitchen on an almost industrial scale. This saved the prison a good deal of money and pleased the Governor immensely.

On one particularly gloomy morning Leanne was to be found as normal in the vegetable garden. It had rained steadily throughout the previous night and it was slippery underfoot. Leanne slipped on a steep slope and cried in agony as her ankle broke with a sharp crack. She lay in the mud, waiting for help to arrive, clutching her rapidly swelling leg and gritting her teeth to combat the pain.

The prison did not have the facilities to deal with such injuries, so Leanne was taken to the local hospital several miles away.

The Governor reasoned that she was most unlikely to attempt escape with such a serious injury and in any case she could not walk unaided. So it was that Leanne Lane came to be in a trauma ward in the local hospital, due to reside there for three weeks. The doctors couldn't do anything until the swelling had gone down and only then were they able to scan the injury. She had broken her ankle in two places. Eventually they operated and set the ankle as required, but she was forced to remain in bed for two weeks. No handcuffs were used as she obviously couldn't move and the doctors had insisted that they be removed for the duration of her stay. She had no visitors. She was of course accompanied, but only by one guard, a female prison officer named Ruth, because she was not thought to be a danger. For Ruth the assignment was a welcome break from the drudgery of her normal routine; a welcome relief from being inside the prison and she relaxed noticeably as the days passed.

Leanne noticed that Ruth had caught the eye of a ward clerk who made a point of being close to her as often as possible. It was obvious to Leanne that Ruth was attracted to him, not least because of his tight jeans which helped display his best features, but also because when he was close enough he never missed the opportunity to display his tactile nature. To Ruth and her newly found suitor Leanne became almost invisible and that suited her.

Ostensibly, Leanne spent her time concentrating on reading the books she had borrowed from the touring hospital library trolley, but, being female, she was able to multi-task and her brain was working overtime. Ruth's distraction and less than attentive attitude were easy to spot and the kernel of an escape plan was born. Leanne realised that she could use her accident to its best advantage, along with Ruth's new love interest. She had noticed that afternoon visiting was when staff took the opportunity to have a little downtime and made themselves as scarce as they could. This often resulted in an increased level of controlled chaos.

On one particular Tuesday afternoon the ward was more than usually frenetic.

The woman opposite Leanne was 91 years old; in fact all the women patients were older than Leanne. They were therefore by dint of their very age much more demanding and difficult.

The woman refused to wear her hearing aids and thus couldn't communicate with her fellow patients other than by smiling and waving at every opportunity. She had regular visitors with whom she communicated in the same way and visiting time was often reduced to farcical levels of hand waving, smiling and other gestures. She also had an inordinate number of phone calls, which were an absolute waste of time for all concerned. Whenever she thought she was not being heard, either on the phone or in person, she resorted to shouting and repeating the same thing over and over again. "I didn't expect to be here you see. I simply came in to see the doctor as I couldn't stand without my knee giving way and they said to me 'you will be having an operation.' I was most surprised. You see I always said that after the age of 90, no more operations and here I am at the age of 91 and they are talking about another operation."

That entire story was the sum total of her verbal communication and was repeated ad infinitum to anybody and everybody.

Another woman called for a commode just after the tea lady had done her rounds. This resulted in patients and visitors, who were enjoying refreshments and biscuits with their loved ones, being treated to most unfortunate noises and an all-pervading foul smell.

One woman had just been admitted with a broken hip and was due for her surgery the next morning. She was therefore a nil by mouth patient by the time of afternoon visiting. She had loudly refused to remove her bracelets and wedding ring as her husband had given them to her, so all her jewellery was covered with sticky tape. She also thought the doctors would steal the items and loudly shared her thoughts with all within earshot. She said she had been married for 59 years to the most wonderful man on earth. She described him as an Adonis. Almost as soon as that description had flown from her lips the most unattractive pipsqueak imaginable settled into a chair at her bedside.

Another of the ward's residents was a rather confused old lady. She had oxygen fed to her through a tube inserted into her nose which she found difficult and uncomfortable. She repositioned it constantly, so that it was often at the top of her nose which meant the oxygen blew into her eyes. She was therefore constantly blinking. She would talk to the other patients, explaining that "Joan is dead, and I'm finishing the sewing for her." She went through the motions of sewing with a needle and thread, gradually sewing all round the edge of the top cover of her bed. As she made progress with her sewing she slowly gathered more and more of the cover up her body, piling it up on her lap. She stopped occasionally to thread the imaginary needle and managed the whole process with her eyes shut, presumably due to the oxygen blowing into her eyes. Eventually the nurses came to her aid as she had no underwear. She was totally exposed but at least she had finished Joan's sewing.

There is little dignity in being ill and even less when a person is elderly and in hospital.

Meanwhile Ruth had taken the opportunity to disappear with her Ward Clerk to a convenient nearby office. They had drawn the blinds in order to get to know each other better. Before leaving Leanne's bedside, presumably in preparation for her tryst, Ruth had visited the toilet and that was when she made her mistake. Her mobile phone sat on her chair. Leanne seized the opportunity. She removed the SIM card, inserted her own and tapped in the number. By the time Ruth returned Leanne had re-inserted the original card, replaced the phone on the chair and was peacefully reading a book. Leanne noticed that Ruth took her phone with her when she got up to meet the Ward Clerk and smiled to herself.

-4-

Billy was surrounded by lions. He was walking alone along a flat, grassy path which ran down the middle of some open and overgrown countryside. The path was narrow and the bushes dense on each side. He had neither seen nor heard the pride stalking him, and the hungry cats had stealthily worked themselves into position. He stood no chance. The lions gradually closed the trap until Billy froze with fear as he spotted the lead female ahead of him on the path. She stared at him with eyes that became narrow slits as she laid her ears back. He heard rustling on each side, but didn't dare to take his eyes off the spectre of death a few steps ahead. He was aware that he was sweating profusely and shaking uncontrollably. There was a single tree ahead of him. He knew it was too far away, but he had no choice but to try. Taking a deep breath he launched himself into a sprint and lunged upward at the lowest branch. He thought he had made it but, in an echo of John Lomax being pulled back in mid air from going over the bridge, he felt himself being grabbed from behind.

He was drenched in sweat and shaking with fear as he jolted awake at the insistent trill of his mobile phone.

"Hello Billy."

Billy looked at the caller's details on the screen. He ran his hand through his hair and licked his lips to try to get enough moisture to speak. He was pulling away from the terror of the nightmare as he tried to clear his head and regain his senses. He was certain he was bleeding from a wound to his thigh, but discovered it must have been the last act of the horror and was only sweat running down his leg.

"Hello, Mum."

He was beginning to emerge from that halfway stage between waking and nightmares.

"Billy, Listen. I can't talk for long, so please just listen. I'm in hospital..."

Leanne briefly explained her situation and finished by saying, "we can sort this out. You need to get in touch with you know who. He can help."

The call was disconnected, but Billy had understood perfectly. He had ended the call by telling his mother that he would let her know, but inwardly he knew he was at a loss as to how he could help her. He could simply ignore her plea and let her stay where she was; he could visit her and reassure her that she would be better off accepting her situation, even though it would entail another round the world trip, or he could contact Ray Quinn or John Lomax. He wasn't even sure he wanted to do anything. At the end he had been firm with her in order to demonstrate that there might be nothing he could do, but he had heard her whimper in the distance as he had removed the phone from his ear and it wrenched at his heart.

He became aware that he was still shaking violently and had locked his grip on the phone so tightly so that he couldn't put it down on the table. His head swam and he felt nauseous. In an unwitting pastiche of John Lomax, he poured himself a large whisky and lost himself in his thoughts. Eventually, emotionally drained, he fell asleep in his chair and the glass gently slipped from his fingers and fell softly to the carpet, spotting it with the remaining drops. As the spillage dried on the carpet so the nightmare was upon him again.

The day following Leanne's covert phone call to her son, she was sitting in her hospital bed chatting amiably to her guard, Ruth. They had become quite friendly, or as friendly as the situation allowed. For her part, Ruth was appreciating the break from prison routine and was enjoying her liaison with the Ward Clerk. Leanne had promised not to betray her to her employers and there was an implicit understanding between them. Ruth would slip away for opportunistic meetings with her newly found lover, whilst Leanne would press the alarm bell at her bedside if she needed to warn Ruth to return quickly. In this way Ruth had become more indebted to Leanne as the days passed.

Ruth had been gone for about ten minutes when a visitor appeared at the foot of Leanne's bed. She was an elderly woman who introduced herself as being from the hospital's befriending service.   This, she explained, involved going into wards and seeing if any patients were in need of "counselling" or, indeed, just somebody with whom to chat and relieve the unending tedium. The woman was frail in bearing and gentle of manner. Leanne recognised strength shining through her steely blue eyes, but there was also a sadness which could not be hidden and Leanne understood that she needed to talk as much as she wanted to offer a service. Although not keen on her afternoon being interrupted, she decided not to be dismissive because Ruth would come back soon enough and send the old woman on to her next helpless patient.

"Hello, my name's Molly," she said as she held out her hand in greeting. "Would you like someone to talk to? You look quite lonely all on your own, just laying there."

Leanne looked at her uninvited visitor and reluctantly returned her handshake.

"Actually, I'm perfectly happy by myself. I've got books and papers to read and things to listen to, but if you want to sit awhile I don't mind."

In the coded language of the hospital befriending service that was as loud a plea for company as is ever heard.

"Thank you; I am a little weary. These corridors are endless and I'm not as nimble as I used to be," said Molly. "I'll stay for as long as you want. Just tell me to leave when you're ready and I won't be offended."

"Ok," said Leanne.

"Is there anything you want to talk about?" Molly continued. "Any moans and groans that I could pass on to make things better for future patients? If not, then perhaps you'd like to tell me what happened to you or a little about yourself?"

Leanne stared intently into the blue eyes and said, "I think perhaps you might have much more interesting things to tell me. You wouldn't be interested in my boring life, but I think you have much to tell." Leanne was not going to divulge the details of her life, especially not the latest few chapters.

"Well," said Molly," we are trained not to intrude and to be discreet, so I'll tell you about my own life. I have nothing to hide, you see."

Those last few words seemed to indicate that Molly already knew a good deal about her and Leanne shifted uncomfortably in the bed. Molly reacted by moving from perching on the upright bedside chair to settling herself at Leanne's side on the bed. She seemed to take an age to compose herself before she began her tale. She had already removed her coat, which was draped around the chair, and she placed her old person's handbag on the bed between them.

"My story begins when, at the age of two, I was abandoned by my mother along with my brother, Harry, who was three. Our mother was young, Jewish, and struggling to find employment in 1932. In the end she must have snapped and, in desperation, left us at the roadside. Thankfully we were found and taken to an orphanage in London. Life at the orphanage was no picnic for Harry and me. The regime was strict and children were forced to conform. Breaking any rules always met with punishment. For example, one day young Harry was caught playing with matches. In order to teach him not to do it again, a match was lit and used to burn the centre of his hand. When I refused to sleep, I was often isolated from the other children. The one thing both of us craved was love, but no one in the orphanage showed us real love or tenderness. I have never forgotten what that was like."

Leanne's concentration began to wander and she searched with her eyes for the return of Ruth. Molly, though apparently elderly, was sharp and picked this up.

"I imagine prisoners are punished for breaking rules in strict regimes, even these days," ventured Molly, looking straight at Leanne with her clear blue eyes.

The parallel was not lost on Leanne and neither was the thought that Molly may even know something of her situation. But what was the woman trying to impart? Was there a message that she wasn't seeing? Her attention became focussed again and she motioned with her hand for Molly to continue.

"Being young children we were heartbroken at losing our mother. We longed for her to come and rescue us; but our hope was in vain. I'd like to think that any child, no matter what age, could be rescued by his or her mother, no matter what the circumstances. Oddly enough the reverse has happened to me as my own son has saved me a few times from various difficulties. You have a son, don't you Leanne?"

The question stunned Leanne, who realised that the old woman was not asking a question but was making an assertion.

"Well, um. ......yes I do. He's in Australia and I miss him badly."

Leanne did not know what had come over her to allow this private information to pass to the other woman. There was just something about her that seemed to say 'trust me, I can help.'

Molly, for her part, saw the realisation seep into Leanne's eyes and took her hand.

"I understand your pain Leanne, and Billy's."

Leanne was startled. She had not given Molly her son's name and yet she had just heard her clearly say it. Her hand tensed inside that of Molly.

"Please, go on. You can't stop there. I....I need to know the rest."

Listen carefully, Leanne and you may be helped. Ruth won't be back while I'm here. She's with her Ward Clerk."

"But..." protested Leanne, "she might and I want to hear the rest of your story."

"She won't be back," insisted Molly, leaving Leanne in no doubt. "So...to continue. Some years later I discovered that when our mother tried to visit us, the orphanage forbade it. Mother was only allowed to visit on a Sunday, but no visits were allowed on the Sabbath Day, so we never saw her again. Do you know the pain of that loneliness, Leanne? I think you do. Can you imagine the desperation of a child who is destined never to see his mother again? I think you can, Leanne. What about you? How do you feel about not seeing your son again? I know how I would feel if I could never see my son again. The pain works both ways. It's unrelenting and the sting gets sharper by the day.

But let's press on. At the age of fifteen I left school without being able to read or write, but managed to find employment as a servant girl in a large house. I told my employer, a disabled lady, that I would love to be able to read and write, but the lady showed no interest in helping me. Life was tough as a servant. I had to rise very early each morning to light the fire, and work until late in the evening. One night, filled with despair, I thought about taking my own life. Have you ever reached such depths, Leanne? I think perhaps you may have.

After a few years I decided to go back to the orphanage where I had grown up, and work there as a house-parent looking after the younger children. I fell in love with a young lad, and became engaged. We married and we were blessed with a son. He was, and still is, the centre of my universe. He is the reason I live. Can you say the same, Leanne? Is Billy the centre of your universe? Is he the reason you live? I think the answer to both questions is yes.

Sadly my dreams of future happiness were dashed when my husband died in a road accident. He loved riding his motorbike and in the end it killed him. I've hated bikes ever since.

I struggled for years to bring my son up on my own. Rather than giving up in despair I trained as a State Enrolled Nurse in Winchester, and qualified after two years. The thought then came into my head that perhaps I could try to become a State Registered Nurse. I travelled to a hospital in Hertfordshire for an interview with the matron in charge of training nurses. I told the matron that I did not have the same education as the other girls, but the matron still accepted me for the course. She advised me to spend one hour each evening, learning what I had been taught during the day. I had never worked as hard in my life. Learning, nursing, providing for my son; just holding things together was all I could manage."

Leanne had the beginnings of cramp and struggled to change position in bed.

"I can't imagine how hard it must have been," offered Leanne, "but, please don't take offence. I admire you for what you have achieved in your life and you have my utmost respect, but how is it relevant to me?"

"Patience!" snapped Molly, showing her steel. "Let me go on. I'm on your side. Please believe me, all will be well if you just listen and then do as I say."

Leanne was both quieted and disquieted. This old woman whom she had never seen before had suddenly appeared at her bed in the hospital and related something of her life and had the effrontery to tell her do as she was told! Why should she? What right did she have? What did she know that would turn the tide for Leanne?

Her face must have shown all her emotions because Molly gave her the sort of look that only a senior citizen can give.

"Right! No more interruptions! We haven't got much time now," Molly said. "I took the matron's advice and studied conscientiously. I would lay each text book on the bed and paw over them until my eyes bled and I fell asleep. When the results were released and pinned up on the wall, I scanned down the list of names and to my dismay could not find my name anywhere. Due to my poor education I was used to always seeing my name at the bottom of the list. Nervously I went back up the list again and to my amazement, found my name was at the top of the list with a pass of 92.5%. I couldn't believe it. I was so excited that I moved on to midwifery training in a hospital in Cornwall. After completing that I applied for a nursing job in the Accident and Emergency Department of this very hospital. I worked here until I retired in the 1980's. That's how I can move about this place so easily.

There are so many tales I could tell about my time in nursing, but we haven't the time for all that now. Perhaps another time," said Molly. "There is one I must tell you, though. There was one occasion that I had to minister to a young man who had been involved in a motorbike accident. It's strange how things go round in circles in life. They say that what goes around comes around, and, for me this was it. He was in a lot of pain due to fractures, much like yourself I imagine. Several years later I was walking in the High Street when a smartly dressed young man called out to me. It was the motor bike accident victim, but I did not recognise him due to the transformation in his appearance. Instead of long greasy hair, his hair was cut short and neat. He had replaced his dirty leather jacket with a clean suit. The young man called out to her "My little staff nurse – you saved me!" He now had a new purpose in life as he had joined the army. My son was in the army as well, you know, but that didn't save his life."

"Please excuse me, but I must pay a visit. I'll be back in a minute." Molly lifted herself from Leanne's bed and walked, bent and stiff, underneath the exit sign. Leanne just sat. There was so much to take in, with so much meaning. What on earth was going on?

Her dazed thoughts were interrupted by the Ward Clerk.

"Ok," he said, "let's get you moving."

"Where's Ruth?" asked Leanne.

"She's OK. She'll be along soon," he replied. "Make sure you bring all the things you need," he advised, as he drew the curtain screen completely around the bed and instructed Leanne to change into the clothes he had tossed onto the bed.

"Why? Where am I going?"

"Out of here," was the reply.

"How?" asked Leanne, now fearing for her future.

"By bike," was the reply.

"I hate bikes," said Leanne. "I can't even bend my leg; it's in a cast. The last time I was on a bike I was damn near killed and I wet myself."

"It's the only way," insisted the Ward Clerk, as he swept her into his surprisingly strong arms and hurried off the ward.

He paused only to cast a meaningful glance at Ruth, the prison guard. He was again struck by her resemblance to Leanne. It was if they were sisters. He held her attention for a few moments, savouring the memory of their time together. Ruth disappeared behind the curtain screen and hurriedly arranged the bed and dummy, which bore a remarkable resemblance to Leanne. She then slipped out from behind the curtains and made her way via staff corridors out of the hospital. The time that the Ward Clerk and Ruth had been together had not been spent in amorous entwining, much to the disappointment of both parties, but had been spent in manufacturing the dummy using clothes that Leanne had not noticed had been extricated from her locker. Even her watch had been pressed into use.

Leanne was so dumbfounded by the turn of events that she could only just manage to gather herself sufficiently to pose two questions.

"Who was that was the old woman?"

Her name is Molly Quinn," replied the Ward Clerk. "You might know her son, Ray."

"What about my watch? asked Leanne.

"Oh, I think John Lomax might be able to find you a replacement, don't you?" was the reply.

-6-

The Ward Clerk did not carry Leanne for her entire journey out of the hospital as it would have drawn too much attention. Immediately after leaving the ward he set her down in a wheelchair, which had been carefully placed just by the door and arranged a blanket over her lap so as to hide anything in her lap. He made sure she bent her legs at the knees so that even her plaster cast was covered. To all intents and purposes she appeared to be just another woman in a wheelchair being pushed along endless corridors from one hospital department to another. He added one clever addition to the disguise when he gave Leanne a large folder to carry above the blanket, which was a genuine x-ray folder that patients take from A&E to the X-Ray Department. He also made sure that their exit route took them back to A&E from X-Ray, so that nobody would have any reason to hinder their progress. It was an easy exit for them and she was pushed into a private ambulance which was waiting outside with its engine running. Hospital CCTV, of course, had recorded the entire internal wheelchair journey, its exit from A&E and their entry into the ambulance.

The ambulance drove for about ten minutes until it arrived safely at a pre-arranged secluded spot for its rendezvous with the bike. There was no CCTV to record Leanne, by then suitably clothed in leathers, being transferred to the passenger seat behind The Biker, who was waiting with his helmet already on. The Ward Clerk lifted her gently onto the seat, pushed a helmet onto on her head and patted the driver on the shoulder to signal his departure.

"Hold on tight," advised the Ward Clerk. He was wasting his breathe because Leanne had previously experienced the back seat of a bike and was already holding on for dear life.

The Ward Clerk watched as the powerful machine drove away and disappeared rapidly into the distance. He turned and climbed into the front passenger seat of the private ambulance. Ruth, The Ward Clerk and Molly Quinn exchanged smiles and the vehicle moved silently into the anonymity of the countryside.

No phone calls were made from the ambulance as they could have been traced. John Lomax therefore had no idea as to the success or failure of the escape attempt. Similarly, Billy, far away in Australia, was ignorant of progress. Both paced up and down in their respective homes and neither would settle until it was over.

The plan had been the result of Billy contacting Lomax after having received his mother's call from her hospital bed. He actually need not have bothered because John Lomax had already concluded that loneliness was not a future he could contemplate. He had lost the one true love of his life, and whatever she had done could be forgiven. He had already been thinking of ways to liberate Leanne from captivity and had shared his thoughts with the only person in the world whom he could completely trust: Ray Quinn.

It was decided that Billy should not return to England as it would be far too obvious to the authorities. It was also decided that John Lomax should not be overtly involved for the same reason. It was Ray Quinn who had drawn up the operation and masterminded its execution. His mother's involvement was a nice touch, because she was helping her son to help another mother and her son respectively. She thought it a wonderful connection. The story she had told Leanne in hospital was a complete fabrication devised by Ray's mother herself and she played her part to perfection. She had thoroughly enjoyed herself and had carried it all off with aplomb and style. She was inwardly very pleased with herself at the part she had played and secretly hoped further adventures might follow. She knew the risks, but didn't care. At her age, she reasoned, there was not much time left for this kind of fun.

The Ward Clerk was found by Ray Quinn. He had been in the forces with him before having become, along with many compatriots, victims of government cost cutting measures. He had drifted from one unsatisfactory job to another, never really settling into civilian life. He had jumped at the opportunity to help his old friend Ray Quinn. Indeed, it was he who had made the suggestion to involve Ruth, with whom he had developed a relationship.

Ruth had experienced what is known euphemistically as workplace harassment from one or two of her colleagues at the prison. She had been told it was very much part and parcel of working in such an environment and she should accept such practices without complaint. The final straw had been when the Assistant Governor had locked her in his office and made it very clear what was expected of her. She had only escaped the inevitable by sheer good fortune when the prison alarm sounded as a fight had broken out in the dining room of her wing. Ruth had bottled the incident up for a while, but had quietly resolved to exact revenge. She had been delighted to become involved with Leanne's escape, seeing it as her chance to hit back at the corrupt regime and the loathsome treatment she had received. She had managed to get herself attached to Leanne as her guard in hospital and her partner had inveigled himself into the role of Ward Clerk. Together they taken their real relationship and used it in the hospital as part of building a believable cover story. Ruth had even left her mobile phone on the bedside chair on one occasion and Leanne had seen it as slackness and taken the opportunity of contacting Billy. It was vital to the plot that Leanne did not understand what was happening, so that her actions were at all times real.

The authorities never chased Ruth and her Ward Clerk because the government department concerned received an anonymous document containing photographic evidence of terrible abuse in the prison, both by and of prisoners and guards, particularly involving senior staff. There were even a few examples of such activity proving political involvement. For publicity purposes the police were shown in the press as trying very hard to find Ruth, The Ward Clerk and Leanne but behind the scenes and over a period of time it became old news and the public turned its attention elsewhere as it always does when the currency of a story runs out.

-7-

Leanne was sleeping like a baby. She was more calm and peaceful than she had been for a long while and a prolonged period of restorative slumber was precisely what she needed. John Lomax sat at her bedside, keeping vigil, ensuring that the one true love of his life was not disturbed. He remained there, unmoving, for many hours recalling and reliving the path of their extraordinary relationship. He remembered with wonder when she had walked into his life and stayed for a week. Neither had managed much sleep, but oh what happiness and joy she had brought with her! He had never known anything like it and just being with her after all the heartache and painful vicissitudes of his life, brought the ecstasy flooding back again.

Ray Quinn slipped into the room unnoticed. "Penny for your thoughts," he whispered, as he laid a calming hand on his friend's shoulder.

John Lomax smiled and, without looking away from his beloved Leanne, said "you may be my friend, but that's none of your business."

Quinn smiled, reflecting that almost everything that had happened to Lomax was actually very much his business, but he took no offence at the remark. Their friendship was deeply rooted and had been tried and tested on many occasions. They were completely at ease with each other and their bond was firm. He allowed his hand to rest on Lomax's shoulder, giving reassurance and succour. He was pleased to have been able to bring Leanne back to his friend. The moment stretched and there was peace in the room.

Eventually Quinn gently broke the silence. "We should talk, John. It's time to make some decisions."

The brevity of his friend's words, and the manner of their delivery, moved John Lomax. His friend had always had the knack of precision and the ability to summarise a situation rapidly, which had been nurtured by his time in the forces. It was part of what made him such a wonderful friend as well as a terrifying enemy.

Spiriting Leanne away from the hospital had taken a good deal of planning, as well as a not inconsiderable sum of money. Quinn had also called in a favour or two from the people who had so convincingly played the parts of Ruth and The Ward Clerk. He had deliberately made sure John Lomax had not been actively involved in order to preserve his innocence if ever events took a turn for the worse. All Lomax had known was that he had been taken to a remote house on Exmoor and Leanne was already there and asleep when he arrived.

Lomax stroked Leanne's cheek tenderly with the tips of the fingers of his right hand until she stirred. Her long-lashed eyes flickered into life and she turned to meet his gaze.

"It's alright, my love; you're safe. I'm here," he said.

"Mmm," was all she could manage as she slowly emerged from the depths of deep sleep and an even deeper duvet. She held his hand to her cheek. "Where am I?"

"It doesn't matter, Leanne," said Lomax. "You're safe and we're together. You won't be going back to that awful place."

"What's happening?" she asked. "How?...."

"Quiet now," he whispered as he bent forward to kiss her. "You need to sleep."

"I was asleep," she said, "but you woke me up."

"I know. You need to take this," said Lomax as he showed her the pill resting in the palm of his hand. "It will help you sleep some more."

"But I don't understand. Why wake me up to give me a pill to make me sleep some more."

"Because we need you to get as much rest as you can. We have a lot to do tomorrow."

"You said 'we'. Who else is here?"

"Ray," replied John Lomax.

"That's all right then," she said, before swallowing the tablet with a sip of water.

She settled back into the bed and was soundly asleep within thirty seconds. John Lomax wondered to himself how the mere mention of Ray Quinn's name always produced the desired effect whatever the situation. Lomax had never doubted his friend's talents, but he now realised that his legend and mystique was spreading. Lomax left the room noiselessly, even though it would have taken a herd of elephants to rouse Leanne.

Just outside the bedroom door Quinn was using his mobile phone. "Don't talk, please just listen. Everything is going to plan. She's out and safe. No details; you only need to know what effects you. Everything else is none of your business. We'll be in touch soon."

On the other side of the world Billy Lane clamped a mobile phone to his ear and listened intently to the tinny voice. Ray Quinn disconnected the call and Billy, realising he had been holding his breath in the tension of the moment, let out a huge sigh of relief. Ray Quinn removed the sim- card from the phone, dropped it to the floor and crushed it beneath his biker's heavy boot heel. He would scatter the fragments from the bike as he swept through the countryside. The chances of them being found and put together again were close to nil. On the other side of the world Billy Lane understood perfectly the need to mirror these actions, so that to all intents and purposes their brief conversation had never taken place. It would have taken the facilities of GCHQ to identify it, but they would never become involved. Billy also understood the subtext of Quinn's call and would wait for twelve hours before moving, as previously directed and agreed, at the same time as his mother and John were due to commence their own journey.

"How is she?" asked Quinn.

"Sleeping like a baby," replied John Lomax. "She'll be ok. We've got about twelve hours to get things sorted out."

They spent half an hour putting the final touches to their plan before concluding their business.

"It'll be tight," said Ray Quinn, understating as ever. He knew the scheme would need a modicum of luck but was quietly confident. He had already donned his leathers. "I'll be off then," he said. "Don't worry, it will be fine. Don't forget to get some rest yourself; you'll need all your energy later.

The two friends shared a firm handshake and looked with complete trust into each other's eyes. The Biker had disappeared round the first corner by the time Lomax returned to keep his vigil at Leanne's bedside.

Billy was overjoyed that his mother, Leanne, was no longer incarcerated and desperately wanted her to be part of young Raymond John's life. He could not, however, fathom how that could be brought about. All he did know with absolute certainly was that if there was anybody who could make it happen it was Quinn. He had many reasons to be grateful to John Lomax, and was fairly sure that he would look after his mother, but he did not have the absolute certainty, the total unquestioning belief in Lomax that he had in Ray Quinn. That man was in a different league; a class of his own.

8

By the time Billy received the call from The Biker, he had made a life for himself in Australia, living with the reporter who had knocked on his front door when his mother had secretly visited him asking for his help. They had gradually fallen in love and had been blessed with a son. They named him Raymond John in honour of the two men, Ray Quinn and John Lomax, who had been most influential and instrumental in Billy being able to survive his traumatic history and the ravages of a fractured and torn family background. Billy was relieved when he saw that his son bore no likeness to his own father, Sandy Lane, who had died so ignominiously in prison. He idolised the little boy and was determined that he would have the upbringing that he had missed.

There was one physical feature that Billy had inherited from his father; namely a nose that was not straight and which had, over a period of time, gradually grown more out of line. It caused him breathing problems and gave him debilitating headaches. The fact that hospitals had played such a prominent part in the lives of himself and his mother was not lost on him. He had been mentally scarred by his own childhood experience of hospital and was fearful of what he might encounter again. However, surgery became inevitable as his breathing difficulties and headaches increased and he was also determined to expunge the paternally inherited feature.

After the operation, Billy left hospital with sutures, inside his nose, firmly ensuring the splints on either side of his septum were held in place. The operation to straighten his nose and clear his nasal passages had been declared a success by the surgeon, but he had been warned that the problem could well recur. For his part Billy was pleased with the outcome, especially as it meant he no longer bore that resemblance to his father. In fact, he had also seriously considered changing his surname in order to complete the process of distancing himself from his heritage. In the end he decided to keep the Lane surname and use it as a constant reminder of everything he should avoid in life as well as a motive to cleanse the family name. He was determined not to view it as a millstone.

Billy was instructed to return to outpatients a week later to have the splints and stitches removed. He was delighted to be home and his two year old son was equally pleased to have him back. He sat on his father's knee and giggled mischievously. The youngster celebrated his father's return by grabbing the ends of each splint, which protruded temptingly from each nostril, between his forefinger and thumb. It is surprising how strong even a child as young as that can be and his strength was matched by his speed. He yelled with glee as he yanked at the prize he had captured. Billy also yelled, but not with glee. His yell was accompanied by an eye-watering, red hot searing pain as his son held up his newly captured prizes and expected praise for his efforts. The boy's laughter turned to tears as blood poured from his father's nose and he was dropped unceremoniously onto the unforgiving floor.

Billy's partner, Charlene, was every inch an Australian young woman. She loved the outdoor life and was determined that their son would enjoy the same lifestyle. She had grown up in a cricket loving family surrounded by two brothers and parents who talked of little else. At the first sign of good weather the barbeque would be set up and an impromptu game of cricket sprung into action. These games were highly competitive, as is the Australian way, and no concession was given to the fact that Charlene was a girl. She sported many bruises as she grew, but never complained. She became an avid cricket fan and was no mean performer with bat and ball. Nothing pleased her more than inflicting defeat upon family members or, if that wasn't achieved, she regularly left her siblings with cuts and bruises as the price they had to pay for their victories.

Her fondest memory was when, at the age of seven, she had asked her twelve year old brother to explain the intricacies of cricket. They were both sitting on the lawn in the back garden. He thought for a moment and, recognising the opportunity to display his teenage importance, he launched into the most confusing explanation he could think of.

"You have two sides, one out in the field and one in. Each man that's in the side that's in goes out, and when he's out he comes in and the next man goes in until he's out. When they are all out, the side that's out comes in and the side that's been in goes out and tries to get those coming in, out. Sometimes you get men still in and not out. When a man goes out to go in, the men who are out try to get him out, and when he is out he goes in and the next man in goes out and goes in. There are two men called umpires who stay out all the time and they decide when the men who are in are out. When both sides have been in and all the men have been out, and both sides have been out twice after all the men have been in, including those who are not out, that is the end of the game."

It was the same deliberately confusing nonsense that he had been told by his older brother, so he felt he was passing down family wisdom.

Charlene recognised pretentious rubbish when she heard it and, in common with most seven year olds, preferred a much more straightforward approach to life. She stood up, looked at her brother, told him he was stupid, picked up her bat and whacked him with all her not inconsiderable strength. She left him with a multi coloured bruise on his knee that took quite a few weeks to heal. Charlene was pleased with herself, even though her mother gave her the worst scolding she had yet experienced in her young life. Charlene noted that it seemed to cure his arrogance, so felt it had been worthwhile. For his part, her brother learned his salutary lesson and thereafter afforded his sister the respect she had earned.

Billy had also taken to their lifestyle and was happier than he had ever been at any time in his life. It was a far cry from the shredded remnants of his upbringing with parents who were constantly at war and afforded him little attention. He often thought that the manner of his father's demise had been inevitable and that his mother deserved all that had happened to her. He had, of course, told Charlene everything. He felt it important for them to be completely open and honest with each other and for that to become the central tenet of   Raymond John's childhood.

It was against this idyllic background that Billy had listened to Ray Quinn's phone call. He had understood the message but had no inkling of the subsequent ramifications. He feared his life was about to take another turn for the worse and long buried feelings of helplessness returned. The nightmares came back again that night as well. He woke with a start, sweating profusely just as the lions were closing in. Charlene stroked his matted hair and caressed his face with a concern she had not had to feel before. She knew that whatever it was that had so frightened Billy would also affect her, and she was deeply troubled.

She could not have known how far reaching it was all going to be.

The next morning Billy told Charlene that he would have to respond to Ray Quinn whenever he was next contacted. He explained their options.

"We could stay here and carry on as we are," he began, "but if we do that my mother will never see her grandson or any other children we have. She won't be allowed into Australia, even to visit, because the authorities here are reluctant to grant entry to a convicted criminal, even though the British are not actively pursuing her. Ray has contacts and has put out feelers, but the feedback is negative. Another option is for us to go to England and live there. I'd be able to work in John's jewellery shop and we would be well looked after. John has even said I would take it over when the time came. If we did that my mother would see Raymond John regularly and I know she would be very happy about that. One bonus would be that Ray Quinn would always be readily available if we ever needed help of any sort. That's more difficult if we are here in Australia, though not impossible. He is a resourceful man and a wonderful friend. Another thought is for us, together with John and mother, to move to somewhere else. Again, that is not really on the cards due to the problem of Mum's status, unless we choose a country that isn't too fussy about who it lets in. We have been told that if we did that, Britain would not seek Mum's extradition. It would be a case of out of sight out of mind, I think."

Billy paused in order to discern Charlene's reaction, but she was giving nothing away.

"Of course, I realise that you have your family here and you are all close. If we went away your parents would not see their grandchildren." Billy stopped again. This time he waited patiently for Charlene to say something.

"Oh Billy," she whispered, "I don't want to leave. I can't leave my family and I love Australia, but I know you have a chance to build bridges with your mother. This is so difficult."

As with all families considering such moves, emotional and practical attachments, preferences and conflicts were almost impossible to reconcile. They calculated that they would be financially better off moving to England, as the jewellery business was thriving and had real prospects. They would become part of its success and expansion and Raymond John would have a guaranteed future. Billy would be able to repay Lomax and Quinn for all they had done for him and Ray Quinn would be available should problems arise. It was a ready- made head start. On the other hand would it be better to stay in Australia and fend for themselves, with Charlene's family close as well?

Neither Billy nor Charlene said very much that morning. There is a difference between a comfortable quiet and uneasy one, and it was the latter that had insinuated itself between them. Each was worried about the other and both were concerned to make the right decision for their young son. Billy knew the phone would ring before long and it would be Ray Quinn wanting an answer, so he needed to resolve the impasse more urgently than Charlene. As far as she was concerned, they could take their time, so she was in no hurry.

When the call came the ringtone meant different things to each. For Billy it carried an urgency and an implied threat. He knew a decision was wanted immediately if John, Leanne and Ray were to have the time to make their plan work even though he had not been told very much. Ray had told him 'that's none of your business," when Billy had tried to elicit further details about the plan, and he steeled himself to be more determined to get the answers he needed. As far as Charlene was concerned it carried no such urgency or threat, it even sounded softer to her as it represented an opportunity to find out more and have further discussion. She was perfectly prepared to talk to Quinn and Lomax if necessary and she wanted time to sound out her own parents. It boiled down to the difference between action and prevarication.

"Hello Billy," said Quinn. He waited for a reply.

"Hello," said Billy. He said nothing else as he waited for The Biker to move the conversation forward.

"Please listen, Billy. Things have changed. I need you here as soon as you can. Don't bring anybody else. I need your help.

There is a ticket for you at the airport in Sydney; the plane leaves in three hours. This is serious."

Billy was stunned. Ray Quinn was not a character easily rattled, but something had obviously happened to unsettle him and now he was asking for Billy's help. He could not envisage any situation in which he could help Ray; it had always been quite the reverse, so something must indeed be serious.

9

Billy joined the moving mass of arriving passengers at Heathrow as each collected luggage from the various carousels. He had fought for and won a prized trolley, successfully fending off competition from other tired and aggressive travellers, and hefted his luggage aboard. He did not know who to look for or what the next few hours and days held for him and was surprised to find Ray Quinn himself waiting behind the barrier. Things must indeed be serious, Billy thought to himself.

The two men shook hands but no words were spoken until they were safely inside the car, which Billy did not recognise. He asked no questions as he awaited news.

"I hope the flight was OK," said The Biker.

"Not bad," replied Billy. "As long and boring as ever, but made much better for being in First Class. Thank you for that."

"No problem," said Quinn. "Charlene and the boy OK?" He asked.

"Yes thanks. He's growing so quickly, it's hard to keep up. So much energy. Charlene sends her regards and is looking forward to meeting you and John," said Billy.

"That will have to wait," Quinn responded sharply.

Billy looked across at him as he drove and tried to discern what was happening, but Ray Quinn's face was a mask.

"I have things to tell you, Billy," said Quinn.

Billy said nothing; preferring to wait for whatever was coming. Quinn noted the young man's silence, taking it as a sign of growing maturity.

"John's in trouble and we need to sort it out," Quinn began. "Your mother and John are now happily together and safe, so that's not the issue, but it's been difficult to get them to that point. Like most things in life the problem revolves around money. The jewellery shop is thriving, but it's not producing sufficient for our purposes. John's solution was to become involved with the local drugs business, but he failed to discuss the matter with me beforehand. The result is that he got in deeper than he could handle. I only found out when things went pear shaped. I discovered him at home with a needle hanging from a vein in his arm. He had been left for dead and it was meant to look like suicide, but I got there just in time. To cut a long story short, he owes money to some very nasty characters. I have made some enquiries through my contacts and by myself, but progress is slow. These people are well hidden, well protected and not particular about who they hurt. I cannot sort this out on my own, which is why I called you. Between us, and with your mother's help, I think there's a way to settle the matter and come through it in the clear. Before we do anything, though, you need to rest. I'm taking you to a hotel. I want you to sleep off the jet lag and then call me. Sorry to insist, but I need you alert and flying from the other side of the world, however much you slept on the plane, isn't good preparation for what we have to do."

Quinn drew up outside the hotel and accompanied Billy to reception. He made sure Billy was safely ensconced in his room before returning to reception. He found the Duty Manager waiting for him.

"Thanks for this," Quinn said. "Let me know immediately if Billy or Leanne or John leave their rooms and if they make any phone calls."

"Certainly sir," replied the Duty Manager, with a twinkle in his eye. "Your wish is my etc.," he said as he bowed to his former commanding officer and smiled knowingly. He wasn't about to seek information as to what was going on. The less he knew the better it would be for him if things went wrong. It was, after all, none of his business.

Ray Quinn had put Billy in a room two floors below John and Leanne. He had arranged for all meals to be taken in their rooms and for their landline and mobile calls to be monitored. He did not want them to get together until he was ready. He was using them as bait. He found himself a dark corner in the lounge bar and waited. He hoped nothing would happen, but he had a nasty feeling, a premonition, that this night would be significant.

And so it proved.

Quinn's senses were on full alert. He glanced at his watch again and noted that it was still only eight fifteen. He was a patient man; something learned from his time in the forces and he was quite prepared to wait for as long as it took. He sipped his coffee and blended into the scenery. Nobody paid him any heed, which was exactly as he wished. He knew he would have to make his coffee last and that he may have to order quite a few more, as he snapped open his newspaper and began to attack the crossword. There were doubts in his mind, which was unusual for him. He hoped he would be proved wrong and that his three "captives" would remain in their rooms for the entire evening and throughout the night.

He was so engrossed in his deliberations that he almost missed Billy walking into the room and sitting at the only available stool in front of the bar. Billy looked around nervously, but failed to spot Quinn. The Biker hoped Billy was only doing what so many lonely hotel guests had done for time immemorial: seeking solace at the bar and, perhaps, the chance of an opportune meeting. Quinn looked around the room and was struck by something odd. The couples around him, and there were a few, seemed ill-matched. The comfortably anonymous mix of blond wood, brushed steel and pale blue leather upholstery made the bar of the hotel perfect for any assignation: business or pleasure or a combination of the two. Also, he noted, there were no groups of people and he would have expected at least one or two company gatherings or birthday celebrations.

"Billy?" The girl who approached was slim and attractive with thick, chestnut hair and eyes the colour of dark chocolate pools. Quinn was luckily positioned such that he could hear conversation at the bar whilst remaining unnoticed.

"Yes," he heard Billy reply.

Quinn was on full alert and he had to make a real effort to appear to concentrate on the crossword. He had no doubts that she was what is euphemistically labelled "escort." Quinn felt a deep sense of disappointment in Billy. With a brief smile that left her eyes untouched she tottered on ludicrously high heels to take a seat on one of the squashy blue sofas, crossing her long tanned legs and waited for Billy to join her. For a moment Quinn half wished he was Billy. It would be so much more simple. Quinn scanned the room, not allowing his eyes to rest on anyone for too long. His attention was rapidly drawn back as the brunette had risen to her feet and was engaged in animated discussion with another man. This man was a rough diamond, unshaven with collar-length dark hair, in jeans and a well-worn leather jacket, the Harley-Davidson logo stretched across his broad back. The body language was pure agitation, and he seemed to be giving her a hard time about something. At one point he grabbed her arm but she wriggled free. Even though he suspected she was capable of looking after herself the old fashioned values that he held dear rose to the surface and he was sorely tempted to cross the room and offer her assistance. It was only the current circumstances that prevented him from doing so. As he continued to observe the developing scene her resistance seemed to crumble before his eyes and, with a last cursory glance around the room, she slung her bag over her shoulder and reluctantly walked back towards Billy.

The whole exchange made Quinn uneasy. He was feeling angry that Billy was letting himself down as he discreetly followed the pair out of the hotel and watched them climb into a taxi. More importantly he was endangering their plans and that could not be allowed. He had trusted Billy and was disappointed that his judgement was awry. He made a mental note to be more dispassionate in future. He also made a mental note of the name of the taxi company and was deciding upon his next move when he spotted the leather jacketed man again, further down the street. Quinn was puzzled and he couldn't decide whether he was perceiving trouble where there was none. He had learned long ago to trust his own judgement and it was telling him to follow the man, but couldn't because he was on foot. That would have to wait as he wanted to catch up with Billy. He walked back into the hotel and, using the Duty Manager's office phone, persuaded the taxi firm's despatcher to tell him where Billy and his newly found lady friend were planning to consummate their brief acquaintance. He made sure the Duty Manager was keeping a watchful eye on Lomax and Leanne and set out in pursuit. As he was driving the car he had borrowed from the ever accommodating Duty Manager his mind was racing. The presence of another woman was a complication he could do without and Leanne and John would not be best pleased. If Billy was stupid enough to jeopardise their plans then he would have to be brought back into line quickly. Quinn threaded a path through the snarled traffic and quietly drew to a halt in an unlit side road close to a seedy looking building. Paint was peeling from the facade and two of the neon letters of its name had refused to light up.

Quinn walked to what passed for a reception and spotted a man behind a desk.

"I need a word," said Ray Quinn, almost in a whisper.

Less than one minute later he exited the front door, armed with the knowledge he required, whilst the badly shaken and ashen faced clerk sat and stared rigidly at the back of the disappearing figure.

Quinn crossed the road and found himself a seat at a table. It suited him that the pub was dark and the bar rowdy and nobody seemed to take any notice of the new arrival. He set his glass down in front of him. He would have preferred something non-alcoholic given the situation, but had bought a pint of Guinness as anything else would have been out of place. He was quietly grateful for the forces training that had taught the finer points of blending in. He had hardly settled into what he hoped would be a short wait for Billy to emerge when his attention was caught by the unmistakable sight of a Harley Davidson jacket disappearing into the building opposite. He hadn't heard the characteristic burble of the engine due to the noise in the pub. The hairs on the back of his neck stood on end and he recognised the signal. He knew trouble was in the air and did not hesitate. Moving quickly he ran across the road and, like a shadow, found his way into the building via the rear entrance that he had earlier stored in his memory. The door was slightly ajar, as it was the same route used by his quarry. Quinn heard the babble of a distant TV as he advanced cautiously along a bare, parquet-floored hallway, alert to any possibility. He silently climbed to the first floor and, controlling his breathing, listened intently.

He eased open the door in front of him and steadied himself for what was to come. He was already imagining the scene. Would he find Billy alive or dead? What of the brunette? What about the mystery man? He visualised the brunette cowering in a corner, her face bruised and bloodied, with Billy standing over her, absolutely rigid with fear. In the event there was no blood, only a sterile and unnatural calm. He scanned the room and his eyes settled on Billy. He motioned with a finger to his lips, ordering Billy to stay silent as he continued to search the room. The brunette sat hunched in a chair, clad only in her underwear, her entire body shaking uncontrollably. Drug paraphanalia was scattered everywhere.

Quinn stood motionless, listening intently for any approaching footfall. There was none and he made his decision. He eased the door shut and moved towards Billy, who quaked before him.

By the time Quinn and Billy left, again by the rear exit and totally unnoticed, the Harley Davidson man lay sprawled on the floor, his eyes glazed and staring, his complexion waxy. The right sleeve of his leather jacket was pulled up to above the elbow and a hypodermic syringe dangled grotesquely from his inner arm, its needle still tugging at the vein. The brunette still sat motionless hunched in the chair, her entire body shaking uncontrollably as her overdose took hold. Quinn offered a silent prayer of thanks that the seedy rent a room that masqueraded as a hotel had no CCTV and was situated in a dark and lonely street.

"I need a word," he whispered in Billy's ear as he propelled him along, gripping his arm tightly. Billy understood the meaning of those words and was more afraid than he had ever been in his entire life.

-10-

Quinn drove back to the hotel in silence. Billy knew better than to say anything. Words would be said soon enough, he knew.

Billy was spirited back to his room and the door was locked. Quinn checked with the Duty Manager, as he returned his car keys, who confirmed that John Lomax and Leanne had remained in their room all evening and had made no phone calls.

Ray Quinn slid the room key card down the groove in the lock and the door clicked open. Despite the late hour, he found Billy wide awake. He had decided it was time to bring Billy to heel, so he told him to sit down and listen.

"I don't know what the hell that was all about tonight," he began," but I didn't bring you back from the other side of the world just so you could play away from home. You have a two year old son and a loving woman and you risk losing them because you can't keep it in your trousers. I brought you back to help John. You owe him. You bloody well owe him! He saved you when you were going off the rails...."

"Actually, he used me for his own ends, if you remember," said Billy.

"Don't interrupt, you ungrateful little shit. How dare you? You stole a watch and John saved you. Yes, he saw an opportunity to get at your father, but he deserved it, didn't he? Lomax loves your mother and she loves him. She's out of prison thanks to us and they're together now, but they still need help. Our help. That means you need to grow up."

"I came, didn't I?" Billy began again.

Ray Quinn was standing over Billy now. "You came because I gave you no choice. I would have fetched you myself if necessary. I told you earlier that John Lomax owes money to some nasty people; drugs people. They don't mess about, Billy. I was afraid they had found out you were in England and I was right."

"You mean you set me up? Used me? Put me out there, knowing what might happen?" exclaimed Billy, incredulous that his supposed protector could do such a thing.

"It was the only way I could bring them out into the open and it worked. I knew they were aware that you'd come back to England. I even knew they had found out you are here in this hotel. I used an escort agency to get the brunette for you, knowing they would recognise the opportunity it gave them to get at you. The man in the leather jacket was sent to kill you, Billy. The brunette didn't know him, but she was promised more money than she could earn in a whole year to lure you to that place. They were banking on the fact that you were away from home, lonely and uncertain. They were right. Your weakness almost got you killed. No matter; I now know what we face, who we are dealing with. Nobody's going to help your mother and John, Billy. They've only got us. The police aren't interested. I have contacts and they'll let me deal with it all provided it doesn't get too messy. From their point of view your mother isn't a threat to anybody and they know she did time wrongly. She's out but they won't spend valuable resources looking for her unless she does something stupid. Also, they'll let us clean up this drugs mess because they know I've got a better chance of success than they have. They can't lose either way. It's win, win for them." It was almost the longest speech Quinn had made in his life.

"You saw how we left that man tonight?" continued Quinn. "That was exactly how I found John Lomax and that was what they intended for you as well. The only difference is that I managed to save John, but that won't stop others coming after him or your mother or you. The only way to end this is to pay them off along with enough of a warning, but Lomax hasn't got the kind of money they're after and neither have I."

Billy was stunned into a prolonged silence. Eventually he asked "but what would have happened if I had 'kept it in my trousers' as you so delightfully put it?"

The sarcasm was not lost on Quinn, and it tested his patience and control, but he remained calm. "They would have tried something else," he replied.

Billy sat and squirmed. He knew he had been weak, had been found wanting and had let Ray Quinn down, but ironically the outcome was exactly what Quinn had wanted. He eventually came to the realisation that Quinn was a very clever man indeed and, rather belatedly, he also came to the realisation that he knew which side his bread was buttered.

"So what happens now?" asked Billy.

"For you, nothing. I want you to stay in your room and wait for me to contact you. If you decide to plough your own furrow again, I won't be responsible for the outcome. Stay here, relax, use room service for your meals, watch TV, recharge your batteries and don't use the phone or your mobile. You may find it boring and lonely, but it's better than the alternative. Believe me, I will know if you do anything other than follow these instructions. I have things to do and

I don't need to be distracted by having to rescue you again. You have my mobile number but only use it in a dire emergency."

"I hear you, but I don't understand what's happening," said Billy. " I know I can trust you, but please don't leave me here for too long. It's the isolation that gets to me."

"I'll be back as soon as I can," replied Quinn. He deliberately avoided giving him any idea of time scale because he wanted Billy to be constantly unsure of when he would return. He hoped that ploy would ensure Billy's compliance.

Ray Quinn closed the door to Billy's hotel room as he left and nodded to the man sitting in a chair just down the corridor. The man, who had been positioned there by the Duty Manager, looked up from his reading, and returned the silent acknowledgement. Both knew that Billy's door had been set to lock automatically and could now only be opened from the outside.

Quinn took the stairs and headed for the room containing John Lomax and Leanne. They had used their forced incarceration much more positively and, when he quietly knocked and entered, he found them fast asleep in each other's arms on a bed which had obviously witnessed much activity and was completely dishevelled. He coughed politely and waited. When there was no response he coughed a little more loudly. Leanne was the first to stir. She lifted her head and raised her arms to run fingers through her hair. In doing so, the covers slipped away to reveal her nakedness. She blushed, smiled and unashamedly sat upright, enjoying his attention. She gazed into his eyes and held them. He returned her gaze for what seemed like an eternity, until he deliberately and slowly let his eyes move from her face to take in the rest of her body. He eventually returned to her eyes and then did not look away, not wishing to spoil the moment. His entire being was taken over by what he was seeing. He was beginning to comprehend some of the reasons for his friend's attraction to her.

Neither of them moved when John Lomax opened his eyes to witness his best friend and his beloved Leanne staring at each other. He gradually took in the scene before coughing politely to break the moment.

"I need a shower," said Leanne. She didn't bother with covering up as she rose from the bed and padded across the room, preferring to revel in the admiring eyes that she knew were following her progress, before disappearing into the bathroom.

Quinn forced himself to concentrate. "Billy has helped us today," he said, "and we need to move quickly."

John Lomax was appreciative that his friend had not referred to the scene they had just witnessed. Both knew that complications would follow and it would have to wait.

"Somebody made an attempt on Billy's life today," said Quinn, "but I've managed to make sure he won't try again. I'm going to take you there now because I want you to understand fully what we are up against. Leanne will have to stay here until we get back."

The Biker failed to mention that it was he who had used Billy as bait and set him up, or that Lomax and Leanne were being used in the same way. If he had told Lomax that, then it would be very difficult to make sure he carried on co-operating, much as he might trust and rely on Quinn.

They waited for Leanne to reappear. This time, much to the disappointment of both men, she was wearing a hotel bathrobe.

"So what happens now?" she asked. She couldn't know that Billy had asked the same question only minutes before.

Ray Quinn answered her with an echo of his reply to Billy, omitting only a few phrases.

"For you, nothing. I want you to stay in your room and wait for me to contact you. Stay here, relax, use room service for your meals, watch TV, recharge your batteries and don't use the phone or your mobile. You may find it boring and lonely, but it's better than the alternative. Believe me, I will know if you do anything other than follow these instructions. I have things to do and I don't need to be distracted. You have my mobile number but only use it in a dire emergency."

Leanne was taken aback by his change in tone and attitude.

"I don't understand what's happening," she said, "I know I can trust you, but please don't leave me here for too long. It's the isolation that gets to me." Another echo.

Like mother, like son reflected Quinn.

"I'll be back as soon as I can," he said. Again he deliberately avoided giving any idea of time scale because he wanted her to be constantly unsure of when he would return. He hoped that ploy would ensure Leanne's compliance.

Leanne noticed that he had not referred to both of them returning, but decided not to pursue the point.

Ray Quinn closed the door to the hotel room as he and Lomax left and nodded to the man sitting in a chair just down the corridor. The man, who had been positioned there by the Duty Manager, looked up from his reading, and returned the silent acknowledgement. Both knew that Leanne's door had been set to lock automatically and could now only be opened from the outside.

-11-

"Do you know him?" asked Lomax, as he and Quinn stared down at the inert body of the man in the Harley Davidson leather jacket.

"Not exactly," replied Quinn. He then went on to recount the events of the previous few hours, finishing the story with himself entering the hotel room occupied by Leanne and John Lomax. Again, he stopped short of dealing with the embarrassing detail of Leanne's performance. "What does this look like to you, John?" he asked.

Lomax thought for a while and considered the scene. They were in a seedy room in a run-down hotel in a dubious part of town, a man's body, a needle hanging from a vein, drug equipment, and a stoned young woman, clad in only her underwear, totally oblivious of all around her.

"It looks like they were here for obvious reasons, which also included drugs. He's dead, probably from an overdose. I can't tell whether he injected himself or she did, or perhaps he injected them both. So it's accidental, misadventure, murder or suicide. Whatever, the result is the same. An overdose for both; one fatal and one will possibly prove lethal," said Lomax.

"Ok," said Quinn, "does it look like anybody else was here, before, during or since?"

"Oh, come on Ray," said Lomax, "I'm not a detective."

"Try," said Quinn.

"I can't see anything that points to that. If anybody was here, it could have been the clerk from downstairs. Perhaps he wanted some of the action and it all went wrong. No doubt fingerprints and DNA will sort it out," said Lomax.

"Indeed they will," replied Quinn, wondering whether his friend had been astute enough to realise that the only man wearing gloves was Quinn himself.

Lomax hadn't spotted the gloves issue but he was wondering why his friend had endangered them both by coming back there.

"Billy was here," said Quinn. "The Harley man followed him after he had picked up the brunette in your hotel bar. I followed them all. The girl is an escort that Billy found and she brought him here. I'm very disappointed by him, by the way, and I should imagine Leanne will be as well. Not to mention his Australian love. Ironically, it helped. The Harley man is interesting. You know you owe money to an unsavoury gentleman? Well, this is his muscle. He was sent here to eliminate Billy as a means of warning you of the dangers of not paying up. Now you really understand what you've got into. Sorry, but this was the most effective way of showing you."

John Lomax was deeply shocked. He had suddenly realised that Quinn had obviously set Billy up in order to flush out the enemy and that both he and Leanne were also being used in the same way.

"Remind me to stay on your side," said Lomax.

Quinn took that as a compliment and smiled.

"So, what now?" asked Lomax.

"Well that depends on you," said Ray Quinn. "We need to look at the options, but I don't think we should hang around her much longer."

They departed via the rear exit and found a suitable pub. It was full of workers, lingering before catching trains home, and others with different reasons for their presence, all filling the place to listen to the stand up comics who were hoping to climb the greasy pole to stardom. They found a table, moving in rapidly to stake their claim as two young men rose and departed, hand in hand, for pastures new. They settled themselves and assessed their surroundings, Lomax noticing that his friend was being particularly cautious and alert, which indicated that the situation was serious.

Having satisfied himself, Ray Quinn was about to begin when the characteristic high pitched screeching sound of electrical feedback assailed the crowd from the small stage near the bar. It had the effect of stopping all conversation as people, some wincing in pain, pressed hands to ears and turned to find the cause of the assault. It stopped as quickly as it had begun, and Quinn waited for the buzz of chatter to resume. He wanted to explore the situation with his friend and explain his thoughts about what actions they should now take. He tried to begin again, but the voice of the landlord, amplified to an excruciating level, beat him to it.

"Good evening and welcome once again to our weekly charity night. I know you will give them all a fair crack and show your appreciation in the usual way. Don't forget there's a bucket at the bar for your donations as we raise as much as we can for the local charities. Tonight's charity will be chosen by the winner of the raffle at about 10.30. Please remember to only put money in the bucket; we found some condoms in there last week and I don't want to explain it again to the wife. She's easily offended you know."

"She's tougher than you think," shouted a wag from the rear of the room, "she put them in there herself. She told me you only use the small ones!"

"Speaking of tough old birds, here's one now. Please put your hands together for our very own Annie Hall." The landlord was pleased to hustle from the stage.

This drew a roar of approval and a round of applause, and the tone was set for the evening. The microphone was handed to Annie, who was in her seventies if she was a day. She was dressed to kill, and wearing as much war paint as a native red Indian.

"I went to the doctor's with my old man Jack the other day," she began.

"Did you leave him there?" shouted a heckler.

"Shut up and listen; you might learn something," Annie replied quickly. "You were born with one mouth and two ears. There's a reason for that."

"Anway, as I was saying, before I was so rudely interrupted, I went to the doctor's with my old man. The doctor examined him all over and told him he was in good health. He asked my Jack if he had any questions. Jack said he did and told the doc that after we have sex..."

"At your age? That's disgusting!" The crowd was warming to its task now.

"I'm still young enough to teach you things you've only ever dreamed about," replied Annie, "see me after if you're up to it; which by the look of you, you're not!"

The heckler leaned against the bar and went back to sipping his pint.

"So, Jack's told the doc that after we have sex he feels cold and chilly. He then says after the second time (this drew a prolonged ooooh from the room) he feels hot and sweaty. The doc called me in and gave me the once over. He told me I was in good condition for my age (another drawn out oooh from the crowd) and asked what Jack could mean. I said it was obvious. He's cold and chilly the first time because it's January, and hot and sweaty the second time because it's July."

She waited for the laughter to subside before launching into another tale.

"So," Ray Quinn began, "let's sort this out."

He was conscious of the fact that they may be overheard and had lowered his voice almost to a whisper. Lomax had to move closer and strain to hear. Annie Hall was in full flow now and their conversation was interrupted by bursts of laughter and clapping.

"Billy is safe and being watched, so I don't think we need worry about him for a few hours. I've also made sure Leanne is safe. She's also being watched. Again, provided she does as I asked before we left, she will be ok," stated Quinn.

"Was that really necessary? I can understand you being careful about Billy, especially in view of how he has behaved since arriving, but Leanne was with me all the time," Lomax was hurt by his friend's treatment of his beloved.

"Yes, it was," replied Quinn. "I know she's been with you all the time; that much was obvious! However, she could easily try to contact anybody when you're not there with her. I particularly don't want her to speak to Billy. They'd only put two and two together and come up with who knows what number. No, we need to deal with this together; just you and me. What we get up to is none of their business, but you know it will be in their best interests. Besides once this is all over I want you and Leanne to live happily ever after and Billy to be able to return to his own utopia down under."

"Don't patronise me, Ray," said Lomax.

"I'm not; really I'm not. I'm just making sure all our ducks are in a row. Believe me, we are not up against amateurs. These people mean business," Quinn was in business mode himself.

"So, what's the plan?" asked Lomax.

"In short, you haven't got the money they're chasing you for. The amount will increase with every passing day because they see it as loss of face. They'd prefer to have the money, but will get rid of you, or worse, as an example to others if necessary. They inhabit a murky world and reputation means everything to them. If they can't get to you, they will go after the people closest to you. You made the biggest mistake of your life when you got involved with drugs. You don't understand how it works and you're not equipped to cope with it. It's vital you follow my instructions to the letter." Quinn ended his speech by holding his friend's gaze with an unyielding stare.

"My plan involves raising enough money to get them off our backs and then giving them a warning of our own so that they leave you alone for ever. After all, I do have my reputation to think of as well," Ray Quinn smiled at Lomax. "One day, when this is all over and peace has broken out, I'll let you into a secret. It will help you understand everything that has passed between us since the day we met when you saved my life."

Lomax was about to ask but Quinn cut him short. "Not now. Not until it's all over."

Lomax studied his friend's face and knew better than to pursue the matter. The silence between them was short and the moment was filled with electricity.

Quinn broke it. "I intend to pay them using their own money," he said.

"Surely that's a dangerous game," Lomax put in.

"Yes it could be," answered Quinn, "but it has a certain irony and the message will not be lost. There's no other way, my friend."

Ray Quinn extricated a phone from his pocket and dabbed his finger onto the screen before holding it to his ear.

"It's all set," he said, "I need you to give us about an hour in there before you arrive. Usual arrangement. I'll call when I'm done and out."

Lomax thought it strange that Quinn had made the call in public, or, more significantly, in front of him. He couldn't hear any reply from within the phone. It wouldn't have mattered if he had because the only response to Lomax had been "ok, no problem."

"Right," said Quinn, "let's go."

"Where?" asked Lomax.

"Back to that lovely room," replied Quinn.

Lomax hoped he meant the hotel room in which Leanne was now residing at her leisure, but he realised that wasn't what was meant when they approached a familiarly seedy building and entered via the same rear entrance through which they had exited a short while ago.

"Don't touch anything," ordered Quinn, "just stand in the middle of the room and let me know if you spot anything which seems odd or out of place. Nobody will disturb us."

Lomax knew better than to ask how he expected them to remain undisturbed. He would have understood more if he had seen the desk clerk slumped and tied in a dark cupboard apparently sleeping like a baby, with a needle dangling from a vein in his right arm.

As they entered the building Quinn caught a whiff of something; an unwashed smell. He was about to open his mouth to warn Lomax when he noticed the grimy rim around the collar of a man's white shirt.

"How long have you been on duty?" Quinn asked the shadowy figure.

"This is my third straight shift," came the reply. "My wife has locked me out so I had to sleep in the car. I've been waiting for you for a long time. I'll get a shower after this is over."

"Good idea," said Quinn with feeling, making an effort at shallow breathing.

Taking the hint, the figure moved away, further into the shadows. "I'll check out the rest of the place," he said. "Oh, you'll need these," he added. Throwing Quinn a small polythene packet he left the room, speaking into his lapel radio as he went.

Quinn opened the packet and squeezed his hands into the tight latex gloves, grateful that he was not a vet.

The shadowy man reappeared. "We're on our own," he confirmed, tactfully keeping his distance. "No sign of life, and we've got one hour."

"Good," said Quinn.

Taking care not to disturb the syringe, he slid his hand into the inside pocket of the Harley jacket and retrieved a soft leather wallet. It contained a hundred and thirty pounds in notes, along with a variety of credit and debit cards and a photograph of Billy Lane. Turning it over he saw a phone number. He'd been right, the man had been after Billy. Quinn was in no doubt the cards were in false names, so there was no means of identifying him. That did not worry Quinn because he now had the phone number he needed. He rummaged around in the man's jacket and trouser pockets and found what he was looking for.

He looked at the phone's screen and saw that a message had been received. It said, "all done?" The sender's number matched that which was written on the back of the photograph. Ray Quinn knew the question was asking whether Billy had been dealt with, along with the brunette.

Quinn thought for a moment and entered, "all done. No problems." He wanted to let the anonymous texter know that Billy and his brunette escort had indeed been dealt with. He did not anticipate any further message and was thus surprised when the phone lit up again.

"Ok, move on. The next one's tomorrow. You know what to do."

Quinn thought for a few seconds before typing "Ok. Time?" He waited, hoping that he hadn't blown the chance of making progress.

"Midday," the text read, "let you know where tomorrow."

Ray Quinn smiled a satisfied smile and pocketed the phone. He now knew that Lomax and Leanne were safe for a few more hours. It gave him leeway; time to plan.

-13-

"I bet this is a prime area for burglaries," said Lomax, his hands firmly planted in his pockets to prevent him inadvertently touching anything.

"Definitely," said Quinn, "and we'll use that. Plus this place is used by escorts to entertain their punters. Up market, it most certainly is not," he added grimly. "You see that camera up there in the corner? I'll bet you a pound to a penny it's used to record the action and blackmail the poor punter. That desk clerk confirmed as much before he decided to inject himself into oblivion."

If Billy is on the recording, we'll need to get hold of it before it links him to matey's demise," suggested Lomax.

"You're right, of course," said Ray Quinn, but it's going to save us a hell of a lot of trouble as well." He left that thought hanging in the air and turned his attention to the wallet, in which he had now found a folded page recently torn from a newspaper. Flattened out, Quinn recognised it as the column for 'Personal Services', well- thumbed and with several of the numbers emphatically ringed in black ink. He wondered if one of them was for the brunette.

Something stale invaded Quinn's nostrils again. The shadowy figure was back peering over his shoulder. "See," he added helpfully, "what kind of sad so and so gets his sex out of the paper?"

"The kind that is there before you," said Quinn, keen to link the Harley jacketed man to the brunette and this seedy room and thus distance Billy from any connection.

"You might be right," came the reply, but it was not convincing.

"Look," said Ray Quinn, " I don't mean to be difficult, but aren't you supposed to be watching out so that we are not disturbed? We'd be happier if you left us to it. This is not your business, and the less you know the better it will be for you."

Suitably chastened, the shadowy man returned to being shadowy and Lomax and Quinn were grateful that the stale smell left the room with him. Quinn made sure he had gone, before taking a silver wrapper from his pocket and partially hiding it between cushions on the sofa.

"That should help convince them," he muttered.

"Just one wrap?" queried Lomax. "Not much of a party."

"It'll be enough for our purposes," replied Quinn, as he moved across the room and turned on the TV. It provided a distraction to the bleak silence of death.

Satisfied that he had arranged the scene in sufficient detail he motioned to Lomax and they slipped away from the building as silently and unobtrusively as they had entered it. The shadowy figure watched them leave and settled down for another long and tedious wait.

His sojourn was interrupted by a knock echoing at the door, followed rapidly by the entrance of the police surgeon. He was carelessly dressed and bleary- eyed. The shadowy watcher, recognised him from other cases, and wondered enviously whose bed he had just vacated. Why was it that when your own love life was on hold everyone else seemed to have it on tap?

"She's young enough to be my granddaughter," he said.

It was said so quietly that the shadowy watcher thought he must have misheard. He hoped that the thud of his jaw hitting the ground wasn't audible.

"Granddaughter? he asked."

"That's right," the unkempt surgeon turned to face him, a wicked grin spreading out across his face.

"I never had you down as a granddad," said the watcher truthfully.

"Neither did I," the surgeon replied evenly. "But some things are out of our hands, aren't they?" and with a minimal lift of his eyebrows continued his work. Subject closed.

After a suspiciously quick and cursory examination of the Harley man's body, as well as that of the by now deceased brunette, he announced that overdoses had done for them both. Satisfied with his pronouncement, he snapped his case shut and strode away, presumably to restart whatever activity had been so rudely interrupted.

By the time the surgeon had left, Lomax and Quinn were seated at the same table in the pub as they had vacated when Annie Hall was holding court. Quinn had arranged for two of his friends, dressed like himself and Lomax, to take their seats immediately they had left. Their drinks, two pints, were even drunk to the same level in their glasses. The CCTV picked up neither their leaving nor their return. It was badly positioned anyway, and there were many standing bodies between it and the two men. Even if it had picked them up, the room was so dark, with the main light shining on the stage throwing shadows around the room, that recognition would have been impossible.

"Ok," said Ray Quinn, "that's Billy's first problem sorted out. The phone number and text messages are a real bonus."

He made two quick phone calls; one to each of the Door Manager's men standing watch in the corridors outside the rooms occupied by Leanne and Billy. Both confirmed that neither of their charges had ventured out or made any calls. In fact neither had even ordered any food or drinks. All seemed quiet on the western front.

Ray turned his attention back to his friend. The bar was still a frenzy of raucous laughter and good natured banter between stage and audience. Annie Hall had been replaced by a man in his mid thirties who engaged in attempting to educate the crowd.

"I want to tell you about some little known facts. Did you know, for example, that in the 1400's a law was passed in England that a man was allowed to beat his wife with a stick no thicker than his thumb. That's how we get 'the rule of thumb'.

"I've got a better measure!" shouted a man from the back of the bar, the announcement laced with innuendo.

"That's what you think!" retorted the woman standing beside him as she smashed him over the head with her rolled up umbrella. "My rule's much more use 'cos it keeps me 'ead dry an' all."

This was greeted with a huge round of applause as the chastened man blotted blood from his scalp with a bar towel.

"Did you also know," persisted the man on the stage, "that if a statue in the park of a person on a horse has both front legs in the air, the person died in battle. If the horse has one front leg in the air, the person died because of wounds received in battle. If the horse has all four legs on the ground, the person died of natural causes. Next time you're wandering around London, have a look."

"My wife's often got both legs in the air!" yelled somebody from the crowd.

"That's because you're about to die in battle, mate." The retort was quick and drew another round of applause.

Ray Quinn allowed himself a smile before bringing them both back to reality.

"Before our Harley jacketed friend decided to move to another realm I had a quiet word with him. He kindly agreed to pass me some helpful information," he said.

Once more, John Lomax knew better than ask for details.

"He told me the name of the man who is chasing you for money and threatening your life. He seemed relieved to be unburdened. By the time our conversation had finished he seemed to want a rest and he nodded off to sleep. As you saw, he decided not to wake up. Such a shame; he might have been useful, but I think we had gone as far as we were going."

"Do I know this man?" asked Lomax.

"I doubt it," responded Quinn, "but you may know of him. His name's Jack Noble. He has a reputation for certain unsavoury activities, which I'm sure is well earned. He sent our late lamented friend to deal with Billy. It was supposed to be set up to appear that Billy and his brunette had indulged in vigorous activity followed by an over indulgence in the old white powder. It would have worked if I hadn't followed him and altered his plans slightly."

"That's an understatement," reflected Lomax.

"True," replied Quinn," but that's life sometimes." He let this last philosophy linger, before continuing. "Anyway, he's gone to Scotland for the weekend, so I think we should toddle off and take a look around his place. I'm told it's quite an eye-opener."

The house was in darkness when they arrived. It didn't take Quinn long to disarm the disappointingly inadequate alarm system and close down the CCTV. The motion sensors in each room were also disabled rapidly. Of the four first-floor rooms the most promising appeared to be a small back bedroom that had been converted into a working office complete with computer, printer, scanner and other electronic devices. This room was by far the untidiest and therefore the one that mattered. Papers were scattered haphazardly over every horizontal surface and drawers were pulled open to varying degrees, spilling out diverse contents.

"Somebody's been here already," said Lomax, aware that he was stating the obvious.

"Yes," said Quinn. "It's almost as if he was looking for something, too," he added sarcastically, surprised by Lomax's statement of the obvious. If he had any sense he'd have been looking for an anti-virus program. Look at that,"

Lomax tracked Quinn's gaze to the computer screen. The machine was already booted-up and, as Quinn nudged the mouse, the screensaver cleared to reveal a scene of technological devastation. Rows of data merged and tumbled from the screen, dancing and swirling before their eyes before mutating into giant insects that scuttled off the screen, cackling nastily. Although functionally competent, Lomax's interest in computers pretty well ended there. This was the first time he had witnessed a virus in action, but even he understood the implications. "'Can you stop it?' he asked.

From the doubtful expression on his friend's face he guessed the answer. As he sat down on the swivel chair he wondered to himself why they had found it already turned on and why it had now taken to destroying the data it held. Suspending these questions for a moment he cleared a space to the left of the keyboard and moved the mouse and mouse mat over to it. He tried valiantly to halt the progress of the virus but was fighting a losing battle. Eventually he shrugged his shoulders and began to explore the contents of Jack Noble's desk, looking for any personal papers to help them build a picture of the man.

"Eureka!" exclaimed Lomax, triumphantly holding aloft a single suspension file which had been squeezed between others in the bottom drawer and was labelled 'current'. In it were bank statements and credit card invoices, some going as far back as a year. There were other files in the desk, which contained correspondence and newspaper cuttings. Closing the drawer, Quinn straightened, and as he did so, noticed a filofax that had fallen on the floor, down the side of the filing cabinet. He picked it up and tossed it to Lomax.

"We'll take this as well," he said. "Have a flick through will you while I have a look round the rest of the house. There might be some useful names and addresses."

Unsurprisingly, the remaining four rooms lacked the hi-tech input and were furnished more in keeping with the age and style of the house. Old-fashioned, Quinn would have called them, though the lingering smell of paint hinted at recent decoration. Only one, the master bedroom, was obviously inhabited, although a single bed in the spare room was also made up. Quinn opened drawers and cupboards, but there was no trace of any female apparel, ruling out the brunette as wife or partner, but several wardrobes, including those in the spare room, were full of men's clothes and shoes. There were a couple of suits and some formal shirts but mainly it was casual wear: Next, Gap, fashionable off-the-peg stuff. Reasonable quality but like the leather jacket, most of it well worn. This wasn't a man who lived extravagantly. Some of the sizes fluctuated slightly too, making Quinn wonder if Jack Noble was a man battling with his weight. In any event there seemed far more clothing here than one man could reasonably wear. Quinn picked up the book on the nightstand: the selected poems of T S Eliot.

"'So what was he into?' asked Lomax, appearing in the doorway.

"Eliot," Quinn replied.

"Not a bad choice,' approved Lomax. Leanne likes Eliot and she's told me a bit about his work.

"I didn't know you liked poetry," said Quinn, teasing his friend whilst at the same time acidly implying that a liking of poetry was connected to cross dressing.

"Why would you? said Lomax, ignoring the tacit insult. "Anyway, I don't particularly. This was an 'A' level set book when I was at school. Before putting it back Quinn turned to a page that had been book-marked. He read quietly and was lost in thought. "We'll take this with us as well," he announced. "I think it might be significant."

He gave the book to Lomax and moved on, eventually arriving at the medicine cabinet. He was surprised to find it had a lock on its door, which he thought was unusual for a normal household medicine cabinet in the bathroom, especially as there was no sign of children living there. He quickly dealt with the flimsy lock. Inside, amongst the normal run of the mill cold remedies, he found six white plastic syringes. Quinn thought that was definitely not the normal contents of a family medicine cabinet. Even a diabetic had equipment different to that.

"It's strange," mused Quinn aloud.

"What is?" asked Lomax.

"Well, we haven't found much preparation debris, either here or in that seedy room where Harley man died," observed Quinn. "Granted we found some there, but I would have expected more.

"Unless he buys it pre-packed; the ultimate in convenience shopping, eh" said Lomax.

Something was bothering Quinn. Something didn't sit right and he couldn't pin it down, but he kept his thoughts to himself for now. He disliked the unexplained; it indicated a lack of complete control and he was not used to that. He parked his disquiet somewhere in the back of his mind and consoled himself with the promising information they had collected.

"What's that? Quinn asked suddenly.

"What? I can't hear..."asked Lomax listening hard.

"Sshh!!" hissed Quinn.

He pointed to a low door under the stairs, from which a barely discernible, but very definite, high-pitched keening sound could be heard. Lomax moved towards the door and opened the lock. He turned the handle and was about to peer inside when a battering ram hammered flush into his nose.

-14-

After Quinn and Lomax had left the hotel room, Leanne had gone back to the king-sized bed. Now she stretched lazily and, although the hollow remained where John Lomax's head had been on the pillow, the other side was cooling fast. In the darkness she imagined she saw his shadowy figure as he hastily pulled on his clothes and she wished he was there with her. She remembered him, fully dressed, leaning over and kissing her on the forehead. His unshaven face scratched her skin. Leanne wished he'd shave more often, but lately he had taken a liking to the modern fad of designer stubble. She resolved to talk to him about it at the next opportunity.

She had enjoyed her display in front of Lomax and Ray Quinn, and had not missed the latter's involuntary reaction. She eschewed the hotel's towel robe, preferring to slide into her Japanese silk kimono, John's latest gift. Leanne opened the blinds and relished the view. As part of the city's new and prestigious canal development, the hotel guests enjoyed looking out over freshly painted black and white bridges, magically hovering over the canal that snaked darkly on its journey out of town. She took in the backdrop provided by the pale blocks and tinted glass of the International Convention Centre, today rendered sharp by a burst of February sunshine. She drew herself away from the window and glided into the bathroom. She took a long time choosing gel, shampoo, exfoliating cream and body lotion from rows of bottles and sachets which sat invitingly on a glass shelf. She ran herself a deep, steaming hot bath and gingerly lowered herself inch by inch into its relaxing clutches. If she must wait in that room, she reasoned to herself, then she may as well make the most of it. She sank further into the bath and, resting her head and closing her eyes, she drifted to sleep.

The bathroom door was partially closed, so she neither saw the handle of the hotel door turn nor heard its click as it was carefully pushed open. The Duty Manager's watcher, supposedly stationed in the corridor outside the room and put there to protect her, peered round the door. He had heard the bathwater running and knew his chance had come. After answering Quinn's earlier phone call and confirming that all was well, he had patiently awaited just such an opportunity. He crept toward the bathroom door and was able to see Leanne's slumbering recumbent figure.

He felt in his pocket for the syringe. His gloved fingers wrapped themselves around the implement and he held it out in front of him, preparing to slide its sharp needle into whichever part of her body best presented itself. He knew he should do it quickly. Jack Noble had told him that Quinn and Lomax were on their way, so time was of the essence. He needed to get on with it, but couldn't help himself. He was transfixed by the beauty of the glistening wet body before him and just stood there, gazing and wishing.

Ray Quinn bundled John Lomax into a taxi and left the cabbie in no doubt of the need to hurry. The driver cursed them roundly, saying that his cab was not a bloody hospital, but he nevertheless recognised the chance to make a fast buck. Lomax's nose was pouring blood and was a frightening sight. Quinn had never been phased by the sight of blood; not even when he had been caught in the horror of the 7/7 London bombings. He had found then, and in his time spent in theatre with the forces, that he could deal dispassionately with gore and injury. He knew his friend's nose was broken, but couldn't be sure there was no other damage. The cabby drove across the river Thames, from north to South.

Quinn leaned forward so that his face was visible to the driver through the sliding glass partition. "Now listen," he said, without a trace of annoyance, "I know London, and I know the quickest way to our hotel from where you picked us up, so please don't cross the river when you don't have to. The fare should be £7.50. I'll give you

£10 and you can keep the change, but please don't take me for a tourist or a fool. And don't talk about road works or diversions."

The shaken cabbie eventually dropped them at the entrance to the hotel and Quinn pushed a note into his hand, telling him to keep the change. He also told him that he had taken his licence number, his name and other details and would be in touch. His exact parting words were, "I'll need a word with you later." The puzzled cabbie watched them disappear through the hotel entrance, innocently oblivious of the ominous meaning carried by those words.

Ray Quinn helped his friend John Lomax up the stairs and along the corridor. Lomax was concentrating on catching the blood which was still pouring from his nose and had ruined at least three man sized linen handkerchiefs. Despite his efforts, the hotel carpet was still suffering. Quinn looked up and caught the ominous sight of Leanne's hotel room door. It was ajar, rather than being noticeably open, but he had spotted it.

The Biker was fully alert. He recognised the danger. Gently setting Lomax down on the chair which should have been occupied by the Duty Manager's trusted employee, he made a mental note to discuss the question of trust. He moved quickly on the balls of his feet and glided silently into the hotel room. All his training and experience rose to the surface. His ears strained for any noise and his eyes took in every little detail.

It was too easy. The man's back was towards Quinn and he was totally concentrated upon whatever was in the bathroom. Quinn guessed what held the man's attention so completely. Having seen her beauty for himself, he couldn't blame the man. He was two feet behind him when he saw the needle. Without so much as a heartbeat's hesitation he struck. The man in front of him slumped and he caught him before he could hit the floor. He never knew what hit him, but when he awoke no amount of effort could free his bonds.

For a reason beyond his comprehension his jacket seemed to be stuck to the wooden arms of the chair and the same was true of the seat of his trousers.

"Hello," said Ray Quinn from behind the chair. "I'm sorry to cause you such inconvenience, but you need to explain yourself. Don't bother to fidget; the glue is strong and you can't get up. Have you ever read "Red Dragon?" Perhaps when this is over you should get a copy from your library."

The captive man breathed heavily and his nostrils flared with fear. He had indeed read the novel to which Quinn had referred and the thought terrified him. In that story, the captive hadn't been glued to chair by his clothing; he had been stuck fast by the skin of his naked body. He also remembered that man's fate and he squirmed with sheer panic.

The effect was all Quinn had intended and it didn't take long for him to ascertain all the information he required.

Leanne had heard nothing of the disturbance and her eyes widened in alarm when she saw Quinn standing over the captive figure in the chair. Her kimono slipped from her body and Quinn couldn't help looking. She coolly took her time to retrieve the fallen garment, knowing very well the effect of her movements.

"I'm sorry to have disturbed you, Leanne," said Quinn, trying but failing to avert his gaze. "It seems our friend here decided to change his allegiance and work for the ungodly. There's enough in that syringe to have done you no good at all. He cannot harm you now, but I'm afraid I need to ask him a question or two and you may not wish to witness at first hand the method I shall use. So, please, go back to the bathroom, shut the door behind you and relax. I'll come and fetch you."

"I'd rather stay here," she replied. "I feel safer when you're around. Besides, my imagination will only run wild and I'm sure the real thing won't be as bad."

The captive in the chair heard the exchange, as he was meant to, and his own imagination was working overtime. His eyes widened with fear and he bounced up and down, struggling for freedom.

"Very well, "said Quinn, "but I must ask you not interrupt or interfere. I shall be as quick as possible, but you never know how long these things take. Everyone's different and you can't tell at the beginning."

He turned to the man in the chair and, having placed the syringe just out of his reach on a table, he stood directly in front of him and began his address.

Quinn knew that most people can withstand some degree of pain. Simple everyday dealings with the doctor or dentist bear witness to that truth. There are also some who can resist more severe levels of discomfort, albeit for short periods. The history of warfare and interrogation confirms that. There are also individuals who are at either end of this spectrum, being able to withstand either chronic pain or no pain at all. But Quinn understood the psychology of fear. He knew what the anticipation of pain can do; especially if it involved the expectation of the captive being subjected to the very treatment he had intended to use on another just a few brief minutes ago.

The shattering completeness of the role reversal was not lost on the man in the chair. That man also knew that Quinn could be a most unforgiving man. His head bowed in submission as his resistance crumbled before it had even begun.

"Now, we'll keep it civilised, shall we? I shall be polite to you and I hope you'll return the courtesy. Look at me, please. I only want to have a word with you. I'm sure you have the answers to the questions I am about to ask and I'm equally certain you'll assist me in any way you can."

The formality of the language Quinn was using and the politeness he employed increased the effect of the message. That effect was not lost on the captive. Quinn was conveying to his prisoner that violence was the last thing he wanted to employ, but he most certainly would if necessary. The anticipation of pain.

"Who sent you?" asked Quinn.

"Jack Noble," replied the captive.

"What were you supposed to do?"

"Use the syringe on her," he said, nodding in Leanne's direction.

"Would it have killed her?" asked Quinn.

"I don't know. I was given it just as it is."

"That's not good enough," said Quinn sharply, moving his hand towards the needle. "Perhaps we'll jog your memory."

The prisoner's eyes couldn't help but follow his movement.

Leanne was spellbound. The power exuded by this man Ray Quinn, combined with its controlled understatement, excited her. She was surprised by her own reaction and became acutely aware that it was almost sexual. She couldn't take her eyes off The Biker. Such calm; such power; such total control! She would have done anything he asked at that moment.

"I don't normally repeat myself, but I'll make an exception just this once. I'll ask you again. Would it have killed her?"

"I think so," replied the man in the chair, looking at his captor with red running eyes. "I honestly don't know, but I think there would be no point in Noble sending me otherwise."

"What was Noble going to do then?" asked Quinn.

"He didn't tell me," said the man, desperate lest his answer was inadequate. "But he told me not to leave. He said to stay in the room and make sure nobody else got in."

"Did he tell you to contact him once you had done it?"

"Yes."

"I see," said Quinn, his mind working at breakneck speed. "So he won't expect to see anybody outside in the corridor standing guard."

"I suppose so," said the captive, utterly spent now.

"Then we'll make sure he gets his wish," said Quinn decisively.

Ray Quinn opened the door and called to John Lomax, who was sitting in a similar chair to that occupied by the captive inside the hotel room, nursing his battered nose. It had stopped bleeding, but a livid maroon bruise was starting to swell beneath his right eye socket. The cause of Lomax's discomfort was a terrified woman, who had been shut in the cupboard below stairs. She had seen her chance to escape and exited her prison with all the force of a runaway train. Ray Quinn had not even seen her and Lomax had tried to cling on to her, but had failed. She had not been seen since. Quinn was unhappy about that particular loose end, and had promised himself to resolve the matter in due course.

Unfortunately for Quinn something else had taken place which he could not have foreseen. Before Billy left Charlene in Australia she insisted on knowing where precisely he could be contacted in case of emergency. Billy had argued that he really didn't know, but trusted Ray Quinn. The row was only settled, albeit uncomfortably, after she had reminded Billy of the actual wording of Quinn's text message, which read:

"Please listen, Billy. Things have changed. I need you here as soon as you can. Don't bring anybody else. I need your help. There is a ticket for you at the airport in Sydney; the plane leaves in three hours. This is serious."

Billy had to promise to get the details before Charlene relented. Neither Quinn nor Billy could know that Charlene had persuaded her parents to look after their two year old grandchild in Australia and had travelled to England. She had told her parents that she wanted to be with Billy so that they could assess their options and decide their future. Her parents were sceptical to say the least because they did not wish their daughter and their only grandchild to move so far away. They only agreed to look after the boy on the proviso that they would bring him to England in six weeks time and all the family could enjoy a once in a lifetime holiday together.

Charlene had not contacted Billy before travelling as she was determined to surprise him. As soon as Billy kept his side of the arrangement and texted his whereabouts to Charlene, she jumped on the next plane to London. She entered the foyer of his hotel at the same time as Billy was meeting the brunette. She was so stunned that she stopped in her tracks. Quinn was paying such rapt attention to Billy and the brunette that he had set him up with that he failed to spot anything else. As Quinn and Charlene had never met, they naturally could not recognise each other. The scene was a moment frozen in time; Charlene, rooted to the spot, aghast at what she was seeing and noticing nothing else and Quinn, concentrating on the tableau, failing to notice the change to the normal rhythm of the hotel reception.

The moment was broken as Billy and the brunette left the hotel. They were followed closely by Charlene. Quinn failed to see her because his attention had by then been caught by the appearance of the leather jacketed man. The outcome was a procession which finished in a run- down building which called itself a hotel and which rented rooms by the hour. Billy and the brunette thought they were the first to enter the room, but were interrupted before making any progress by the presence of the leather jacketed man. He had already solved the unexpected problem posed by the arrival of Charlene, by shoving her unceremoniously into a low under stair cupboard, which he duly locked. He could not have known the effect that being in a confined space had upon Charlene. As a young girl she had experienced the same thing and been forced to undergo therapy for over a year afterwards. Thus, when the door to the cupboard closed and entombed her, it had all come flooding back. She was reduced to a quivering wreck in a matter of seconds. She heard muffled voices through the door, but could discern nothing apart from those same voices being raised in an argument. The Harley man had calmly awaited the arrival of the amorous couple and surprised them as they entered the room. He was following instructions given to him by Jack Noble and had been forced to extemporise by the unexpected appearance of a feisty young Australian woman. Charlene made no sound until she entered the keening phase of her desperation. Thinking on his feet he drew a knife, threatened Billy and moved to the brunette to inject her with a lethal dose of heroin. He was about to start on Billy when Quinn entered the arena and finally settled matters.

Billy had not seen Charlene because she had already been locked in the cupboard by the time he entered the room. Also, as she was silent none of the participants were aware of her presence. It was only when Quinn took Lomax back to the scene, after having returned Billy to his guarded hotel room, that her plaintive keening was heard. When Lomax opened the cupboard door it was Charlene who came charging out, like an enraged bull, head down.

She was totally out of control when she smashed into Lomax, broke his nose, and careered out of the room, easily brushing aside his feeble attempt to stop her.

She was thus now one loose end that Quinn needed to resolve.

-15-

Not normally susceptible to self-doubt, Ray Quinn reviewed matters. Apart from the immediate situation in the room in which he had a terrified captive glued to the hotel chair, an extremely shaken John Lomax with a broken nose, a doe-eyed Leanne waiting upon his every word and the very real prospect of Jack Noble appearing at any moment, there was the question of Billy. He was still in another room waiting for Ray, being guarded by another of the Duty Manager's men. Had that man also swapped his allegiance? Was Billy, even now, in difficulty up there? Quinn thought that unlikely because he had used the text message to tell him that Billy had been dealt with at his seedy assignation with the brunette. The question was whether Jack Noble had checked on that? If he had, he would have found his leather jacketed man and the brunette there, both deceased and, more significantly for him, no Billy. Noble would have recognised the scene for what Quinn intended it to be: a warning. Quinn knew it wouldn't stop Noble. In fact he knew it would have the opposite effect. Noble would view it as a challenge that could not be allowed to go unremarked. In an ideal world Quinn needed to keep Billy apart from Leanne and Lomax so that Noble's targets were not in one place. He also needed time to deal with them in accordance with his original plan, but the situation had taken a turn for the worse. Then there was the potential complication posed by the desperate figure from the cupboard. Quinn felt sure it was female, despite not having seen her, but who was she and why was she there in the first place? Who had shut her in that cupboard? Where had she gone and how could he find her now? Leanne also preyed on his mind. She had blatantly flirted with him in front of Lomax and seemed to be giving him a message. He obviously recognised it for what it was, but it was a dangerous game. He wondered if it really was just a game or whether she meant anything more concrete and would see it through. He admitted to himself that the thought wasn't without its appeal, but knew he would resist the temptation. He had a wife, after all, whom he loved. Besides that, he was caught up in a rapidly developing and increasingly serious situation.

He told himself that, just as he always had when out on a mission, he must concentrate totally on the job in hand. He must focus on the desired outcome and ignore side issues. He must be ruthless. He knew he was proficient in that regard.

Sometimes in life one had to adjust, think rapidly and be decisive, he concluded. Perhaps it was time for reunion. Perhaps the lure of just one target would prove too much for Noble to resist. Quinn began to admit that the idea had its merits. He held the initiative, which was an advantage. He was no longer merely reacting to change; he was driving it.

He picked up the phone and entered Billy's room number.

"Hello Billy?" he said. "Have you eaten?"

"No," came the reply. "I've been just sitting here watching TV waiting for you. I was getting worried. The isolation gets to me and time drags. I can't stand it."

Quinn recognised the signs of panic and knew it wouldn't be long before Billy did something silly again. Quinn had specifically instructed him to sit tight, but Quinn knew that if he was left to his own devices he wouldn't be able to resist the temptation for too long.

"That's ok," said Quinn, "the waiting's over. I need a word with you, so let's talk over a good meal. I'll meet you in hotel restaurant in five minutes."

He had deliberately neglected to let Billy know that Lomax and Leanne would be joining them because he wanted to assess his reaction when he saw them sitting at the table waiting for him. Quinn punched another number into the phone and spoke in hushed tones to the Duty Manager. He then turned to address the room.

"So, dinner anyone?" he asked as he replaced the handset. "Oh, I'm sorry," he said to the chair bound captive, "I nearly forgot. You can't, can you. Never mind, we'll try to bring a doggy bag back for you. Meanwhile, why don't you enjoy the view?"

Quinn moved the captive, still glued to the chair, so that he was facing the bedroom window with his back to the door. Having satisfied himself that the gag he had just tied around the man's mouth was tight enough to prevent him calling out, but only just loose enough to allow breathing, he led Lomax and Leanne out into the corridor.

The Biker, Ray Quinn, his senses on full alert, saw it first. The lift was on the move and heading their way. He hustled his charges towards the stairs and told them to wait at the first turn. He climbed back up the twelve steps and carefully positioned himself so that he couldn't be seen. He heard the soft 'ching' of the bell announce its arrival. The only passenger in the lift stepped out. Quinn saw in him an assured confidence, a man who was used to being in control. He was carrying something that was partially hidden to Quinn. The man moved down the corridor and knocked on the door from which Quinn had only moments earlier emerged. There was, of course, no reply from within and the man rapped more loudly and urgently. He became impatient and opened the door quietly.

"Hey, it's me; Noble. Is it all done?

As Quinn could not see into the room he could only guess at what happened next.

"Don't just sit there, answer me!" ordered Noble.

The captive could only wriggle, stamp his feet and twist his head in a vain attempt to communicate with the man who had sent him there.

"What the hell....?" shouted Noble as he saw the plight of his hired muscle.

The glued man was desperate and the chair keeled over as he pushed and pulled in different directions to no avail. He grunted, his nostrils flaring as he hit the floor. He lifted his head in time to see Jack Noble flick his lighter and hold it against the rag which had been stuffed into a glass bottle. Noble tossed the flaming bottle toward the stricken chair-bound man and calmly walked from the room, closing the door quietly behind him.

Quinn saw the flash and heard the 'wumph' as Jack Noble, unhurried and in control, returned to the lift. He watched Noble re-enter the lift but had no time to find out whether it was going up or down. He could only hope that Billy had already left his room and was either in or on his way to the restaurant. He bounded down the stairs towards Lomax and Leanne and told them to stay exactly where they were as he rushed passed them. He slowed to compose himself before entering the restaurant and his eyes sought the table he had booked. To say he was relieved to see Billy sitting there reading a menu would be an understatement. He turned on his heels and found Leanne and Lomax impatiently waiting for him exactly where they had been left. Although he had planned for Billy to be the last to arrive because he wanted to assess his reaction, he was pleased that he now had all three of them safe in one place.

The hotel's fire alarm sounded just as Lomax, Leanne and Quinn sat down, almost as if it had been triggered by pressure pads in their chairs. The evacuation was for the most part an orderly affair. The car park was used as the gathering point and hotel staff checked names against lists of residents. The last people to vacate the building and be checked against the list of residents were an elderly couple, dressed in full wet weather clothing, who emerged from the hotel's entrance foyer carrying their suitcases. The Fire Brigade had arrived within a couple of minutes of the alarm sounding and the

Officer in Charge could be seen giving them a piece of his mind. He had, after all, risked his men's lives by searching for them whilst the fire was taking hold. For their part, they seemed totally oblivious to the danger they had caused and were more concerned as to when they could return to the restaurant to finish their meal. This annoyed the officer even further because it showed that they had left the restaurant when the alarm sounded, returned to their room, packed their cases and donned their outdoor clothing before sauntering from the building. Other residents had evacuated immediately, some even in their nightwear. Thus the delay caused by the couple was doubly annoying because it was cold and raining.

Once the fire had been extinguished people were gathered into public areas in the hotel, but not into the bedroom section in which the fire was located. The damping down process was in full swing, but the room occupied by Lomax and Leanne, now reduced to a smouldering hollow, was being treated as a potential murder scene because the body of a man in a chair had been found.

Quinn overheard the Fire Officer confirm that only one room had been involved, so it seemed that Noble had not torched Billy's room. Quinn had made sure his three charges stayed close to him throughout. The checking of names in such situations is designed to ascertain whether anybody is unaccounted for rather than discovering extra people and therefore it did not reveal the additional figure in the car park. Jack Noble had calmly joined the gathering assembly and, placing himself as close to his four targets as possible without being discovered, watched proceedings with an eagle and predatory eye. Ray Quinn spotted him, but made no mention of it to the others. Quinn had also taken note of the presence of the man designated by The Duty Manager to guard Billy's room. He was standing behind Jack Noble and was whispering into his ear.

"Billy," said Ray Quinn, "was there anybody outside your room when I called you down to the restaurant?"

"No," replied Billy. "There was just an empty chair along the corridor."

"Are you sure?" pressed Quinn.

"Yes, I'm certain," answered Billy.

"Ok," said Quinn.

His mind was racing and it did not take long for him to make a decision.

"I think we should go back to the restaurant. We are not in any immediate danger and I don't know when we'll be able to eat again."

Leanne, Lomax and Billy each looked at their protector with a plethora of questions forming in their minds. Their faces reflected their puzzlement, but Quinn was in no mood for his group to remain standing in the open in deep discussion. He ushered them back to their table. An overly attentive waiter appeared and took their drinks order. Quinn insisted they each decide upon their meal before he would contemplate anything else.

The waiter returned with their drinks and carefully took their food orders. When he departed, Ray Quinn raised both hands in front of him, palms outwards, resting on the table just above the wrists.

"Now," he began, as his three fellow diners stifled their own questions in response to the body language, "let's take stock. How you each came to be here tonight is not important. We'll discuss that another time. It's obvious that this Jack Noble, to whom you owe money John, knows we are here and is upset with you."

"That's an understatement," interjected Lomax, "he's just tried to murder Leanne!"

"And failed," Quinn reminded him. "But he won't accept failure. He need not have torched that room tonight. He could have released his man and perhaps got information about us from him. He chose not to do that. He preferred to torch the room and let the man die an horrific death. He even stood in the crowd outside and made sure we knew he was there. He was giving us a warning. Of equal importance is that he was issuing a warning to everybody else, his own staff included, that failure is not an option. It also lets us know that he will stop at nothing. It's not about money any more, John, it's about respect and loss of face."

Quinn looked at each in turn, studying their eyes. He took his time. He was seeking confirmation of their commitment, but he was also asking for affirmation of their trust. As his gaze fell upon Leanne, she returned his look with a barely perceptible blush and lowered her eyelids in submission.

"Now that we're all together," he continued, "I think you should remain so. There is strength in numbers. I realise it gives Noble just the one target, but he won't be able to pick you off one at a time. Let's enjoy our meal, as much as we can, and restore some sanity here."

"But Ray," queried Billy, "why were you keeping us separated? You asked me to come to London alone as a matter of urgency to help John. You've no idea what trouble that caused, by the way. No sooner do I get here than I'm set up to be killed. On top of that I don't understand my mother's part in all this."

"We've already had that discussion, Billy," Quinn flared. "As I said at the time, there are things that are none of your business." Quinn was now all business, irked by what he saw as Billy's selfishness. "Suffice it to say that we are where we are. We have flushed out John's enemy, given him a bloody nose (if you'll pardon the obvious irony there) and effectively taken charge of the pace and direction of events. He is on the back foot. We are no longer having to react to him; he is now forced to be on the defensive. It's a stance he won't like, so we need to be alert."

There was an authority, recognised by Lomax and Leanne, that brooked no argument.

"Talking of bloody noses, what happened to you?" asked Billy, looking at John Lomax, whose face was growing a multitude of interesting colours, but keeping a wary eye on Quinn's reaction.

"I walked into the edge of a door," said John Lomax, infusing his answer with as much sarcasm as he could muster.

"Actually, I'm glad you've brought that up," said Quinn, looking directly at Billy again. "Obviously, John didn't actually walk into the edge of a door. He's not that daft. There was a door involved, but what lay behind it caused the injury. We heard crying noises from behind a door under the stairs and as soon as John opened it somebody hurtled from the dark depths and smashed into his nose. John tried to grab whoever it was, but he or she escaped. I was looking the other way at the time and so didn't see anything except a fleeing figure. I'm pretty sure it was female. Whoever it was will certainly have a headache by now. We do have one clue though. I found an earring on the floor not far away. I haven't mentioned it to John before, because there's been no chance. Does anybody recognise this?" he asked, fishing in his trouser pocket and producing a droplet shaped pierced earring which boasted a not inconsiderable diamond at its centre.

The earring was passed from Quinn to Lomax.

"That's a very nice piece," said Lomax; "quite expensive." His jewellery shop experience was showing. "Perhaps we'll keep it and I can have a second one made for Leanne when this is all over. What do think, my love?" he asked as he passed it to Leanne.

"Well," she said, "it's a lovely thought, but whoever it belongs to will certainly want it back. It's beautiful."

She placed it carefully in Billy's palm and let go reluctantly. He looked at it and slowly closed his fingers around the gem. He closed his eyes to hide his tears.

134 | P a g e

"That belongs to Charlene," he whispered. "I gave them to her when our son was born. But I don't understand. How did it get onto the floor in that room?"

Ray Quinn was on the verge of losing what little patience he had left with Billy.

"When will you ever learn?" Quinn asked through gritted teeth. "I asked you to come over to help John and I specifically told you not to bring anybody with you."

"But I didn't!" exclaimed Billy.

"Then how did she know where to look for you?" asked Quinn.

"I sent her a text, but I didn't for one moment think she'd come all the way here. She must have left the boy with her parents," responded Billy, his face reddening with shame.

"For heaven's sake, Billy! It's hard enough helping your mother and John without having to be a babysitter for you as well. Now we've got to find her. You better pray Jack Noble doesn't get to her before we do."

"So what do we do now? asked Billy.

"You need to be very quiet while I think. Don't even consider interrupting. Don't even breath loudly. Can I trust you to do that? I need John with me and I need Leanne to start playing her part. But you? What do I do with you? Unfortunately, you're the only one of us who will recognise Charlene, so you'll need to be with us. Were it not for that fact, I'd put you away in a place so remote that nobody would ever find you. So just tread very carefully, Billy."

It was as clear a warning as Ray Quinn had ever issued to anybody. Normally he used understatement as a means of stressing the import of his message, but he was at the end of his tether with him.

-16-

Some situations demand radical solutions and The Biker considered this was one of them. He had detailed his plan to the others, who had agreed with varying degrees of enthusiasm. The main reason Leanne was keen to play the part given to her was that it would give her the opportunity to spend more time in Quinn's company. She had noticed his reaction to her lately and was also drawn to the power he radiated. John Lomax was grateful that it would mean the end of his present difficulties, a future with his beloved Leanne with sufficient money to support them. Billy's agreement took the form of silent, resentful acquiescence. He just wanted to find Charlene and live happily ever after with their son. For Ray Quinn, it had become a matter of honour and, besides that, he was enjoying himself.

And so it was that he was sitting on a bench by a table outside a pub in Hertfordshire. Dressed in his full leathers with his helmet resting within reach on the table, he had chosen the location carefully, so that he had plenty of escape routes. It had been an easy task to find Jack Noble and arrange the meeting. The latter had responded as he knew he would. Noble was a confident man, not used to failure, and that made him predictable. He would neither refuse the opportunity of making money nor resist the chance to settle a score. Ray Quinn had simply sent him a voice mail with enough of a temptation for him to take the bait. It said:

"We must stop playing games. I have something you need. We can do each other some good, so I need a word." He then gave his proposed location and time.

Jack Noble was intrigued as well as angry. He was determined that whoever this upstart was would soon be put in his place. It shouldn't take long; it was a simple matter of teaching the stranger to have some respect. After all, who was this who was treating him like an errant schoolboy?

He had, however, never been treated to The Biker's "I need a word" invitation, so could not understand its full meaning.

Noble swept into the car park and brought his BMW to a gravel crunching halt in the only available space, which was just out of sight from Quinn's position. He strode towards Quinn with purpose; a man on a mission.

"Hello," Quinn said wearing a relaxed grin, purposely not proffering his hand. "It's good of you to come."

"Let's not play games, whoever you are. I saw you after the fire in the hotel car park, with the man who owes me money. I hope you've got it with you, for his sake," said Noble through tight lips.

"Let's not rush," said Quinn. "Take a seat, have a drink. The least we can do is to be civil to each other."

"Why should I waste time?" responded Noble, becoming visibly agitated. "It's a simple matter. You've either got the money or you haven't."

"How much was it again?" asked Ray Quinn, smiling again at his adversary.

"You've got some nerve!" Noble hissed. "You sit here as if butter wouldn't melt and you think you can haggle with me. Well think again. Who do you think you are?"

"I am the man who can save you from yourself," said Quinn brightly. "I've got the money, but I've also got a proposition. If you accept then I can guarantee you'll make more money than you've ever dreamed of. If you don't then I can guarantee you end up rotting in some cell or perhaps even worse. Now be a good boy, settle down, and listen. You're making a spectacle of yourself."

Noble fought the temptation to throttle this stranger who had the effrontery to treat him like a child and smile whilst doing so. He was struggling with his demons when another car crunched across the gravel. It drove straight into a space that had been vacated only a few seconds previously, not ten yards from the two men. The driver's door opened and a woman alighted. Quinn was struck by her poise and assured calm whilst Jack Noble was struck by her other obvious attributes as she walked towards them, her breasts upon the offbeat. She sat beside Quinn and smiled at him before turning her gaze towards Noble.

"I am sorry to disturb you, but I have an important document that needs your signature," said the woman.

"No problem," said Ray Quinn, studying the paperwork for a brief moment before using the pen offered by the woman. "I am sorry. Excuse my rudeness, let me introduce you. Leanne Lane, meet Jack Noble."

"Pleased to meet you, Mr Noble," said Leanne, "I've heard so much about you," she continued, treating him to her best breathless huskiness.

Jack Noble was speechless. He had recognised her immediately as the woman who had been in the hotel car park after the fire, with John Lomax and the man who now sat in front of him. His brain was working overtime. There was obviously something suspicious going on, but he couldn't work out what it was.

"Is there something the matter?" asked Quinn kindly. A waiter was close by and he asked him to bring a glass of water for his friend who was by now coughing and spluttering. "Perhaps this will help," said Quinn as he handed Noble a plastic shopping bag. Jack Noble wiped his eyes and peered warily inside the bag. He discovered several neatly tied bundles of notes.

"There's half the money John Lomax owes you," said Ray Quinn. Please don't insult me by counting it; that would cause me great offence. I am a man of my word. You will receive the other half in due course. However, if you take the opportunity of joining our little venture this will be as nothing."

"Why should I trust you?" asked an incredulous Noble.

"Several reasons, actually," replied Quinn. Firstly, I invited you to meet here and you are not in any danger. In fact you are safer with me than you'll ever know. Next, I've brought you some money as a sign of good faith. I need not have done that. Then I have obviously kept my word and come alone, showing trust in you that you will not endanger me. Finally, I've introduced you to Leanne. That's a risk on my part because she is John Lomax's partner. I trust you will show her the same courtesy as you have me, because if you don't then the rules change. So as you can see, I've come here in a spirit of peace and goodwill."

Jack Noble took a while to compose himself before asking a question.

"My man in the chair...did you do that?"

"I am afraid so. Most regrettable, but he was a loose end. Call him collateral damage if you like," replied Quinn, with a disarming smile.

"I'm not sure I can view it like that," responded Noble, "but we'll let that slide for a minute."

"No," said Quinn, "we won't let it slide. You don't control this. He worked for you, so he deserved what happened to him. He's gone; so forget him. Oh, and while we're on this subject the other one outside Billy's room at the hotel has decided not to work for you anymore. He's asked me to let you know. Don't bother to look for him; he's far away and not coming back."

Noble sat there with his mouth open in stunned amazement. Who was this man who had come into his life and rearranged it so dramatically? Who did he think he was? Whoever he was he was certainly sure of himself, thought Noble.

Quinn pressed ahead, not wanting to allow Noble any thinking time. He had him off balance and was not going to let him settle. He nodded imperceptibly at Leanne who reacted on cue.

"The first draft of the contract for London is ready on your desk for your approval, and I've confirmed your flights for next week. Mr Lane has booked a table for eight thirty this evening at your usual restaurant," said Leanne, playing her part wonderfully.

"Perfect," Quinn said, nodding his approval. The charade was meant to convince Noble that he was not dealing with lightweights. The use of 'Mr Lane' was intended to catch Noble's attention. He would know that DCI Sandy Lane was no longer of this world, so the only 'Mr Lane' would be his son, Billy. The hook worked. The fact that Leanne had made such an obvious physical impression as well was a bonus and Quinn made a mental note to use that advantage again.

Leanne crossed her legs, making sure Noble saw just enough of her charms, and flirted with her eyes for good measure. It was like taking candy from a baby, reflected Quinn. They had found Noble's weakness.

"So, what's the plan?" asked Noble, without taking his gaze from Leanne. "You've given me half the money your man Lomax owes, but haven't told me how or when I'll get the rest. He'll regret it if he thinks he can con me. People have died for less."

"I am fully aware of that," responded Ray Quinn. "He is not treating the matter lightly and neither am I. You may be assured you'll receive the rest of your money within seven days from today. I do not intend to let you have the details of our further plans until then. We need you to show some good faith as well. I think our meeting is at an end. We'll meet here at the same time on the same day next week."

The money that had just been given to Noble had been raised by Lomax selling some of his jewellery stock at a reduced price. It was, after all, an emergency. The other half of the cash that Noble was expecting had already been similarly raised, but neither Quinn nor Lomax intended to hand that over despite the promise they had just given.

Ray Quinn rose from his seat and motioned for Leanne to follow. If Noble spoke to Leanne next he would know they had their man.

"Will you be here as well?" asked Jack Noble.

It was the same principle as somebody looking backwards over a shoulder to indicate interest after having passed by and The Biker smiled to himself.

Jack Noble watched them leave and waited for his observers to break cover and follow. If Ray Quinn thought things would be easy he would be made to think again. He would let his followers lead him to Billy and correct the mistake. Billy would pay the originally intended price. He took his time leaving. There was no need to hurry because he trusted his followers to ensure Quinn and Leanne Lane did not realise they were being watched. Others had underestimated him before and regretted it and those two would go the same way. He thought it a shame that Leanne could not be saved, but he could not afford the luxury of pity. This was going to be interesting, he told himself, as he climbed into the driving seat of his BMW and buckled on his seatbelt. His mobile buzzed.

"Did you catch it all?" Noble asked.

"Yes, Jack. We've got the lot. Arrangements have been made, as you'll soon see."

He had only been driving for a few minutes when he rounded a bend to see Leanne Lane's car in a lay-by, having been stopped by a police patrol car. He was tempted to stop and offer assistance, but he thought better of it. Now was not the time to derail his plans by becoming involved in a trivial incident. It was probably just a speeding offence or a routine check, he told himself. He slowed to match the speed limit and drove past, hoping not to have drawn attention to himself.

"Hello Jack. Did you see them?" asked the disembodied voice via his Bluetooth.

"Yes. I saw them. That was quick, though. It will give them something to think about. Thanks. See you when I get back." Noble smirked as he drew away, glancing in the rear view mirror as he did so.

As he was looking backwards Leanne was being asked a question.

"Is this your car, madam?" asked the officer.

"Yes," she replied.

"Do you have your driving licence with you?" the officer persisted.

"I'm afraid not," she replied.

"And your name is..?"

"Leanne Lane," she said.

The second officer spoke into his radio, asking for a check on her details. Confirmation came within seconds.

Leanne couldn't help herself. She was still tense from the meeting at the pub, so she began her carefully rehearsed delivery. Talking herself out of difficult situations was one of her specialities, but in the half-minute or so she'd had, she'd already decided to come clean. They must at least have her licence-plate number and had probably filmed her in the act of defying the diversions with closed circuit cameras, although she was staggered that such a petty traffic offence should result in her being pulled over at the roadside.

'I'm really sorry,' she began, apologetic but coolly professional just the same. 'I know I shouldn't keep ignoring the signs, but I forget and before I know it, I'm just way past..."

The traffic officer just looked at her.

"Sorry?" Leanne helped him out. "The diversion signs, I should follow them, I know."

"This isn't about driving, madam." The officer was suddenly floundering, but held up a photo. Leanne glanced at it and was confronted by a face with an obviously broken nose and swollen, multicoloured cheeks.

"Well, I don't remember assaulting a police officer" she began, instantly regretting the flippancy.

"It's nothing you've done, Miss Lane," the policeman persisted, with a touch of irritation. "You may want to sit down," the officer indicated the back seat of his car and more from surprise than anything else, she did as she was told. "This man was found dead a couple of hours ago."

He may as well have punched her in the stomach, and for several seconds her whole world seemed to sway.

"No!" Leanne blurted uncontrollably. "No, he can't be."

A sudden vision flashed through her mind of another occasion many years ago when, as a young teenager, she had got home from a party to find police in the house and her mother crying uncontrollably. Her father had been killed in a road accident.

"When, how?"

She was so sure that this couldn't be right.

The second officer had taken out a small, black notebook. "We'd like you to help us identify him. Would you like one of us to be in the car with you?"

"No, thank you. I'll be fine. I'll follow you."

She felt the first creeping chill of apprehension as she allowed herself to consider the seriousness of what she'd been asked to do.

"'Right," she said, "let's get this over with."

As soon as she got back into her car she used her hands free set to call Ray Quinn.

"Hello Ray. You were right; Noble cannot be trusted. I've just been pulled over by a couple posing as police officers. They showed me a photo of a man with a broken nose and swollen cheeks. It looked like John, but I don't think it was. I'm supposed to be following them to the station to identify him, but I don't think they intend to take me there."

Quinn listened intently.

"Can you see this through?" he asked.

"Do I have a choice?" she asked.

"Not really," replied Quinn, trying to sound reassuring, but not certain he was succeeding. "Ok. You'll be fine. They won't hurt you. Stick with it. I've got Mr Noble with me and I need a little time to have a word with him."

17-

Ray Quinn disconnected the phone and turned to Jack Noble. He smiled pleasantly at him, but his eyes betrayed his true feelings. He was still fully clad in his leathers, but had removed his helmet.

"I'm sorry I've not had time to dress properly for the occasion," he began, but events have moved on apace. It's unfortunate," he continued, "that we seem to have come to such a situation. It appears your people have Leanne whilst I have you. I am prepared to wager the entire sum of money contained in that plastic bag I gave you, that your BMW had brake trouble and you couldn't stop running into that tree after our meeting at the pub. I'd chase your garage if I were you; BMW's are not supposed to have such faults. They're not cheap, after all. I hope the car's not too badly damaged; trees can be so unforgiving. I really didn't want to ruin the car, I only wanted a word with you, but time was against me, so it had to be a sledgehammer to crack a nut, so to speak. Such a shame you had to park it out of sight at the pub, you just can't trust anybody these days, can you? I'm sorry it has come to this, but I had to take precautions, you must understand that."

Quinn was leaning comfortably against a chair directly in front of his adversary, who was having trouble clearing his aching head and getting his eyes to focus. "No need to get up and shake hands," continued Quinn. "Try and relax," he said, "it will all become clear in a few minutes. Please don't waste your energy trying."

Jack Noble's senses were indeed returning and his situation shocked him. He was stuck fast to a chair, in exactly the same way as his man in the hotel room before he had torched it. In addition this man Ray Quinn was mocking him, taunting him. Nobody had ever had the effrontery, much less the courage or stupidity, to do that before. He was quite literally puce with rage but no amount of struggling made any difference. Quinn watched patiently until his fury ebbed away.

"May I welcome you to our humble abode?" he asked, the mockery increasing. "It's not much, but it will suffice for now. After all, we haven't got much spare cash now that you seem intent on bleeding us dry. I need to talk to you about that. In fact I need to chat about a few things. We might as well begin with money."

Noble's body shook with anger and his eyes blazed. He couldn't speak as his mouth was full of one of his own rolled up socks. He therefore had one foot fully clad in sock and shoe whilst the other was bare. His eyes took in this detail.

"I'm sorry about that, "apologised Quinn, "but I need to make sure we don't disturb the neighbours. Just a nod or shake of the head will be enough. Do you understand?"

Noble stared fixedly at The Biker without moving. He knew this was a test, to make sure his resistance had been broken. He neither nodded nor shook his head.

"Now that's not very polite," said Quinn as he moved a bowlful of water close to Noble's bare foot. "I'm sorry the water's a touch cold, but we haven't sorted out the hot water system yet. Never mind, it will serve to make sure we don't stain the carpet, won't it?" He produced a pair of bolt cutters from beneath Noble's chair. "The state of your nails! You really should look after yourself better, you know. Perhaps there will be no need shortly. Shall we try again? I don't normally repeat myself, but it seems I've had to do so a fair bit lately. It's a bad habit; I really must stop it. Now, do you understand? A nod for yes and a shake for no will do."

Quinn's hand moved slowly toward the bolt cutters and Jack Noble felt an unmistakable stirring within his lower abdomen as resistance flowed from him like water rushing down a drain. His head nodded furiously.

"That's better, Mr Noble. You'll notice I'm still being polite even though you don't deserve it. I always think that manners maketh man. Decorum at all times. Don't you agree?"

Noble had come to the conclusion that he was being held by a madman, and his head nodded furiously. His feeling was confirmed when Quinn rolled up a rag and stuffed one end into a bottle so that it was just soaked with the liquid contained therein. The bottle was carefully placed upright on the table beside him.

"Do you recognise that?" asked The Biker.

Noble nodded.

"Thought you might," said Quinn. "I thought at the time it was a touch clumsy; not precise enough. Why ruin a perfectly good hotel room? I'll try to resist that temptation, though it's quite appealing at this present moment. As I said, welcome to our humble abode. We haven't been here long and we don't intend to stay once our little misunderstanding has been cleared up. Now where was I? Oh yes; money."

Raving lunatic, thought Noble, trying not to show his thoughts.

"I gave you half the money my friend John Lomax owes you. He is a man of his word as am I. I told you the other half would follow in seven days' time, but you didn't appear to understand the message. That promise still holds. However, the rules have changed somewhat. Mr Lomax is not at all happy that your people appear to have kidnapped his beloved Leanne. Notice the words I use, please. They indicate the depth of feeling he has for her and reflect the lengths to which he will go to obtain her freedom. It goes without saying, of course, that she must be unharmed. Not so much a hair must be touched or a scratch be inflicted, even accidently. Both Mr Lomax and myself are quite clear on that. May I take it that we can agree upon her immediate release, in exchange for your good self, obviously?"

Jack Noble knew he had no option and nodded wearily.

"Good," said Ray Quinn. "That wasn't so hard, was it? I'm pleased we haven't had to lower ourselves to unpleasantness."

The necessary arrangements for Leanne's release were agreed. She was brought to the flat, apparently none the worse for her ordeal and Jack Noble was given his freedom. It had been a deliberate act on Quinn's part to allow Leanne's captors to bring her to the flat because he wanted them to know where to find her. He wanted Noble to trust him. He would test that trust later.

After Noble and his two men had departed, Quinn looked at Leanne with questioning eyes.

"I'm ok," she said. "Not a scratch. I really did think they were policemen for a while, though."

There was a disturbing silence between them and Ray Quinn began to feel uncomfortable in her presence. He was worried she might refer back to their significant moments of eye contact and was relieved when John Lomax and Billy walked through the door.

"Thank God that's over," breathed Lomax as he hugged Leanne tightly.

Quinn, Lomax, Leanne and Billy spent the whole of the next day at the flat finalising plans. They agreed on the following:

1/.   The need to find Charlene.

2?   The need to raise money.

3/.   The need to settle with Jack Noble.

4/.   The need to return Billy and Charlene to Australia in one piece.

5/.   The need to arrive at a situation that would mean Lomax and Leanne could live undisturbed.

"So that's it then," said Quinn smiling at his own understatement. It's all very easy really. It shouldn't take much doing. Let's have a meal, drink some wine and relax. Get as much sleep as possible tonight and the fun will start in the morning." The Biker's eyes were sparkling.

They laughed nervously. Experience had taught them that whenever Ray Quinn was in this mood significant events were about to occur. They were all tired and nobody had any trouble getting to sleep, after their meal and wine. They closed their eyes, each knowing that others ought to be restless that night.

-18-

Billy was the last to make his appearance at the breakfast table. He looked exhausted.

"You look awful," said Leanne.

Billy nodded and smiled weakly.

"He ought to be tired," Quinn put in, with a smirk.

"Is there something you want to share with us?" asked Lomax.

"Cross out point number one on your lists," said Quinn. "Even as we speak Charlene is sleeping peacefully. She managed to text Billy last night and we fetched her. She's a little embarrassed about your nose, John, by the way."

"So she should be," said Lomax, gently rubbing his soreness.

"I think it's improved your looks, actually," ribbed Quinn.

"Hmph," was all Lomax could muster.

"I'm glad she's with us now," continued Quinn. We're all together and that makes it easier to control."

"It also makes us an easier target," put in Billy.

"Yes it does," said Ray Quinn, so we'll have to be that much more careful. Now, let's move on to the other items on our list. I think we can deal with point number three with Charlene's help. Leanne, take

Charlene to the library this morning. We need information about Jack Noble from its archives. Anything you can dig up might provide vital clues as to how to deal with him. I intend to use whatever you find against him. We need to reduce his power and influence in the city; to show others that they too could stand against him; to undermine his standing. Apart from that, Charlene needs to be given something useful to do; something to get her out. She's already showing signs of rebellion at being cooped up indoors. Being shut in the dark under stair cupboard has traumatised her and I can't have her being fragile. Being a careful man, Quinn insisted that Charlene and Leanne used a transmitter and tracking device so that Charlene would always be located. While you're doing that John, Billy and I are going to deal with the money side of things. Jack Noble hasn't learned his lesson yet, but by the time we're finished he'll be looking forward to early retirement.

Charlene proved an imaginative and insightful researcher. She found a good deal of information about Jack Noble, including newspaper cuttings, local authority searches, microfiche records of criminal activity and court papers, financial details and some tax records. Leanne settled at a desk to examine what Charlene had brought to her. She was so engrossed that she didn't notice time passing quickly. When she eventually realised that Charlene had not been to her desk for quite some time, she placed her hand on the paperwork to keep her place and raised her head to look around. Charlene was nowhere to be seen, so Leanne rose to her feet and scanned the entire room. There still no sign of her. She was annoyed and wondered to herself why both her son Billy and now his betrothed shared a propensity to disappear at difficult moments.

Leanne's initial calm began to accelerate into concern and towards mild panic as she realised that Charlene wasn't within sight. Leanne had not considered the possibility that she would ever really walk off without her, but now she'd done it. Why the hell hadn't she insisted on her wearing the tracking device? The transmitter button was burning a hole in her pocket when it should have been buried somewhere within Charlene's clothing. Leanne swept her eyes up and down the library, desperately seeking out Charlene's familiar clothing. At one point she thought she saw her flapping coat tail, but it was only a middle-aged man scratching himself in concentration. She'd covered the whole of the fourth floor of the library but Charlene wasn't in evidence. The escalators were tucked into one corner of the building and Leanne felt sure she wouldn't have had the time to get that far, but now she had to consider the possibility that she must have. The problem was, had she gone up or down? It would be impossible to search the whole six-floor library herself, so she approached the library desk.

"I'm sorry to disturb you," she said, trying to keep the tremor from her voice," but I need some help. I've lost my daughter."

"Oh, I see," said the woman from behind the desk. With a minimal hand signal she beckoned to a uniformed security guard. "This lady has lost her little girl, can we do a search?"

"No," Leanne interrupted. "She's not a child, she's a grown woman, but she's a bit upset at the moment and is a stranger to this country. I have to find her."

"Don't worry, madam, this happens all the time. We'll soon find her." The guard was reassuring. He activated a button on his walkie-talkie. "Put out a missing person, please," he said and relayed the description Leanne provided.

Meanwhile Leanne went shakily to the main library reception area from where, she had been told, the search would be coordinated and to where Charlene would be taken when she was found. She waited for an agonising fifteen minutes, at the end of which the original guard came back to her shaking his head.

"We've looked everywhere. She's not in the building. Would you like us to call the police?' Leanne was at a loss. Why would Charlene suddenly wander away when she had been warned that she must stay with Leanne.   She didn't know what to do and was about to phone Lomax when, by the main doors, she caught sight of something sparkling on the floor. Trying to maintain her composure she scurried across and picked up the teardrop shaped earring. It had an expensive looking diamond at its centre. Leanne recognised it at once. She felt as if someone had walked over her grave.

"Are you alright, madam?" asked the guard who had by now appeared at her shoulder. Would you like me to call the police?"

"No," she blurted forcefully. Realising the guard had baulked at her reaction, she tried to calm herself and said, "no, thank you, "it's kind, but I'll do it. I know who to speak to."

Outside the library, and away from the guard's hearing, she took out her mobile phone to call Ray Quinn. Before the call was connected she realised that she should be phoning John Lomax and entered his number instead. Was she becoming infatuated with Quinn? she asked herself.

"Hello. John. Thank God you're there! I'm at the library. We found a lot of good stuff, but I've lost Charlene. I've searched all over, but...." Leanne's words tumbled out in a garbled rush.

There was a deafening hiss and Lomax's voice was drowned out by a wave of interference. Leanne waited for the static to clear. It didn't and there was no other option but to terminate the call. She would have to move to somewhere else and try again. But before she could, her phone rang again.

"Thanks for ringing back," she began.

There was some more interference.

"Is that Leanne Lane?" The unfamiliar male voice was sharp and cutting.

"Yes?" she said.

"Let me reassure you your daughter in law is safe and well."

"What? Who is this?" Leanne grappled for understanding. What was going on?

"Don't worry," the man reassured her. "As I said, she is perfectly safe, but she's going to stay with us now, because you have something that we want."

"What do you mean?"

"Why don't you just listen for a moment, and I'll tell you how you can ensure her safe return." Leanne tried to place the accent. She thought she detected a trace of Welsh, but wasn't sure.

"It's very simple," the voice went on. "As soon as we have finished this conversation, I want you to take your phone and drop it in the black rubbish bin five yards to your right, just so that you won't be tempted to use it again to dial 999."

Leanne looked across to her right. About five yards away was an ornate, cast-iron bin. Whoever he was had her in his sights. He was right there with her. She scanned the crowd of people around the square. Everyone seemed to be hurrying to the shops, back to the office, in and out of the nearby museum. She could see no-one talking into a phone.

"All right,' she said, trying hard to keep her voice steady. "What do you want me to do?"

"I want you to go back to the library and gather up all the material you have been working on relating to Jack Noble. Then go to your bank and withdraw the amount of money that John Lomax still owes Mr Noble. I know the bank will say they cannot release that amount without at least 24 hours notice, but you will just have to be persuasive. We know you have the money in an instant withdrawal savings account, so don't let them fob you off."

"But what's going on? asked Leanne.

"That's none of your business," came the reply, "and if you know what's good for you you'll make it stay that way. Make sure you don't leave anything behind in the library. I know what should be there."

"Then what?" asked Leanne, fully focussed now.

"Go to the Conference Centre. Sign in as a delegate. There's only one presentation there today. The receptionist will give you a pack. Ask her for a spare, because you have a friend who can't attend and you've promised to pick up any materials. Go into the hall, sit two rows from the back. Empty one pack and put the materials under your seat out of sight. Put the library stuff and the money into the empty pack. Stay for ten minutes and then leave. Make sure you leave the pack on your seat. Go to the coffee shop on the corner and sit down. Order a coffee and wait for my call. When we're satisfied that we have everything we need, I'll call to let you know where you can find Charlene. Don't make any attempt to contact your friends or involve the police. If you do I won't be able to guarantee her safety. The same will be true if you try to evade us or do anything to draw attention to yourself. You are being watched. Do you understand?" The caller's voice was barely a whisper. "I hope you appreciate how serious I am."

"How do I know you'll do what you say?" asked Leanne.

"I don't think you have a choice, do you?" the chilling voice replied, before the line went dead.

She had been through a great deal in her life, but could not remember feeling as alone as she did at that moment. Charlene had not wandered off, she'd been abducted. She had to do as she was told. Sick with fear she gathered up the materials from the library and hurried towards the bank, dodging other pedestrians as she forged her way through. Someone was observing her, following her, but she dared not look back. Leanne had to resist the urge to grab someone, another woman perhaps, and plead with them to call Lomax or Quinn. She kept an unnatural distance from everyone she encountered.

At the bank there seemed to be an unusually large number of people queuing to carry out their business. The line moved agonisingly slowly and Leanne had to overcome the urge to shout "hurry up!" or barge her way to the front.

Ray Quinn shifted uncomfortably in his seat. He made a mental note not to buy that particular make or model when the time came for him to own a car. He had hired the vehicle to help maintain anonymity because he had driven a hundred miles each way to sell the drugs to a well known dealer. He had made sure the car was the same make and model as that owned by Jack Noble, and had also taken the precaution of using forged licence plates. To anybody casually looking it was Jack Noble who had made his regular journey on the usual day at his normal time. He hadn't actually met the dealer because he always used a different runner as a precaution. The drugs he had sold had been stolen earlier from one of Noble's own runners. The overall outcome pleased Quinn. Jack Noble had been deprived of a significant amount of gear which had been sold to his usual contact for the normal price. Quinn was therefore in possession of much more money than they needed to pay Noble the last half of what Lomax owed. Quinn would keep his word by paying Noble with money raised from the sale of his own drugs. There would be a great deal left over, which they would use to put back the cash that Lomax had earlier raised by the sale of some of his jewellery stock and make sure Lomax and Leanne were able to live without financial worry for the foreseeable future. It was also sufficient to return Billy and Charlene to their domestic bliss in Australia and still leave a tidy sum for himself. It was a very neat arrangement, thought Quinn. Very neat. He felt even more relaxed about the situation because he knew, from high up inside police sources, that a decision had been taken to turn a blind eye whilst he solved the Jack Noble problem for them. They were happy as long as he was careful. He smiled as a motorway patrol car passed in the opposite direction and flashed its lights. The automatic number plate recognition would have pinged, but they officers had obviously been told to ignore it.

Traffic on the motorway had been light, but had built up as he approached the city on his return journey. It was moving at an uneven, caterpillar pace and he was beginning to develop cramp in his right leg. He also needed to pay a visit to the nearest facilities, so he pulled in at the next services. He calculated that Leanne and Charlene would be back at the flat so he made the call. John Lomax and Billy had been left there to hold the fort and keep a wary eye out for any sign of Jack Noble or his workforce. His call was answered almost before it had rung at the other end.

"It's John. I think we've got a problem, Ray. Leanne tried to phone me, but she was cut off. I recorded what she said. Listen. Leanne's alarmed voice sounded in Quinn's ear as he heard her exact words.

'Hello. John. Thank God you're there!" "I'm at the library. We found a lot of good stuff, but I've lost Charlene. I've searched all over, but..'

"She was cut off by interference before she could say anymore," said Lomax.

"And she didn't call back?' asked Quinn.

"No, Ray."

"And she was definitely on a mobile?"

"Definitely. The number came up as hers," confirmed Lomax.

"Ok. You two stay there in case anybody comes back. I'm not far away now. Phone me if either of them returns or anybody arrives. Also, let me know if there is any phone contact from anybody at all." Quinn finished issuing instructions and disconnected.

He eased himself back into the driving seat, waited for the Bluetooth to connect and moved off into the traffic. He tapped in Leanne's mobile number. It worried him that it was obviously switched off. As soon as he disconnected, the hands free rang loudly in the car. He was surprised by its volume and, momentarily distracted, he veered out into the adjacent lane of traffic, causing the car coming up alongside to stand on his brakes. The driver hooted and gestured angrily.

If only you knew, thought Quinn. "Yes?' he shouted at the unit set into the dashboard.

He recognised the voice immediately as that of one of his most trusted biker friends. It was Frank, the same man who had treated Leanne to the ride of her life for four hours on the back of his bike and frightened her to death. "I'm outside the library, Ray. I can see Leanne, but she's on her own. She was on the phone for a little while and is obviously agitated about something. I've never seen the other woman before so I wouldn't recognise her. Do you want me to keep an eye on Leanne?

"Definitely, Frank. Stick to her like glue. She won't recognise you because you were in biking gear when you last met. Be careful, I don't want anybody to know you're interested in her."

"No problem," replied Frank, "but I might need support if this Charlene or the opposition turn up."

"Good man," said Quinn. "I'm not far away now."

He disconnected the call and drove on, deep in thought, whilst not many miles away Frank continued his surveillance. He saw Leanne return to the desk she had been using in the library, gather up a good deal of paper and other material, put it into a bag and walk out as nonchalantly as she could. He followed her at a discreet distance to the bank and, having ensured she was in the queue, retreated to a shaded shop doorway across the road. He swept the area looking for anybody or anything out of the ordinary, but saw only normality.

Leanne left the bank a worried woman, not only because of her situation, but also because she was carrying a great deal of cash. She looked both left and right before seeming to make a decision and heading for the nearby Conference Centre.

Quinn was parking the car when Frank called again.

"She's at the Conference Centre. She's carrying the stuff from the library and she's been to the bank, so I bet there's money in there as well."

"Get in there and see if you can see what's happening," said Quinn. "Let me know as soon as you can. I'll be outside."

Frank watched Leanne as she walked to the front desk and spoke to a receptionist who turned an open file round for her. Leanne picked up a pen and wrote something on the page. She was then given a pack and the receptionist pointed with her finger, obviously giving Leanne directions. Leanne was about to walk away as directed but stopped and said something to the woman behind the desk, who leaned across her desk to hand Leanne a second pack.

Frank waited until she was out of site and strode up to the desk. The receptionist began her rehearsed dialogue.

"Welcome to the conference, Sir. If you could sign in please." She turned the open file towards him and he saw Leanne's nervously scribbled name. He signed himself in as Billy Rubin and smiled inwardly. He wondered if anybody would work out the meaning of the name. "You'll need this pack, Mr. Rubin," the woman continued with her intonation. Frank wondered why she had been placed as the first person that delegates would see upon entry. She certainly wouldn't win any prizes for her enthusiasm. She raised her finger, as she had done for Leanne, to point the way.

"Do I need a second pack?" enquired Frank.

"No, Sir. There's everything you need in the one I've given you." She dismissed him by looking over his shoulder for her next customer.

Quinn had arrived just in time to see Frank's back enter the Conference Centre. He settled himself on a wooden bench and awaited developments.

Inside the Conference Hall itself seats were filling quickly. Frank watched as Leanne, following instructions to the letter, sat two rows from the back. She carried out the bag exchange as directed and settled into her seat. He managed to find a seat not far away. Now that he was close he could see her discomfort. Surreptitiously she glanced around to seek out anyone who could be the one watching and waiting. She obviously needed help, but he couldn't risk using his phone to seek instructions from Ray Quinn. He made a decision and the noise attracted her attention. She saw a balding man in a black leather jacket spill the contents of his delegate's pack and kneel to retrieve them. He looked up and his eyes met hers. He gave her what he hoped was an imperceptible but reassuring nod, before gathering his papers and moving off.

Leanne's heart pounded. Who was that man? Why had he attracted her attention? Was it the end of the matter? Should she still do as she had been instructed? She looked around, desperately seeking familiar faces, but she knew she was alone. Her desperation was interrupted by the duo of presenters introducing themselves. Leanne hoped it wouldn't be one of those events where the delegates were asked to introduce themselves as well. "Hello, my name's Leanne and I'm being blackmailed." Now that would cause a stir.

The passage of time seemed interminable as she looked at the clock on the wall ahead of her, but, finally the minute hand hit two and she quickly got to her feet. She left the bag on her seat and walked out of the hall. She half expected someone to hurry after her to point out that she had forgotten the bag, but they didn't. The door closed behind her and she walked across the now almost deserted foyer towards the entrance, her footsteps echoing unnaturally loudly on the marble floor. No one had followed. With relief, Leanne forced her legs to keep moving. She was telling herself that the ordeal was nearly over. Once they had what they wanted they'd let Charlene go. She didn't know whether to be pleased or disappointed not to be greeted by the sight of police surrounding the building. Why is there never a policeman around when you need one? She asked herself the age old question. There was no reason to expect police to be there, but it is a natural instinct to rely on them when all seems lost. Unfortunately, everything seemed oddly normal and the world was going about its business.

Then she caught sight of Ray Quinn sitting on a bench not fifty yards away, seemingly without a care in the world, soaking up the sunshine.

-19-

Leanne's heart leapt at the sight of her saviour and she almost broke into a run across the square. She didn't understand how Quinn came to be there just when she needed him most, but her only thought was to run to him, melt into his arms and feel his strong protection around her. She knew he had seen her but was puzzled by his lack of movement. Then she remembered the instructions she had been given. The caller had been definite and threatening, and she knew she must resist temptation.

She forced herself to concentrate and looked for the coffee shop on the corner. She had to search hard because it was partly hidden by the awning of its neighbouring hardware outlet and a newly erected bus stop. She tried to maintain her composure as she walked towards the inviting aroma of freshly made coffee, but inside confusion, rage and turmoil were winning the day. She imagined hundreds of pairs of eyes burning into her from every conceivable angle, seeking and discovering her innermost secrets.

The last few steps were made on shaking and wobbly legs and she grabbed the nearest chair with the desperation of a late night drunk taking his final fall. A waitress approached and her bored voice began to recite the litany of coffee options. It was the last thing she needed and she switched off, waiting for the girl to finish before asking for something normal. She fished her phone from her pocket and placed it directly in front of her, desperate for it to burst into life. She looked at her watch, but couldn't focus at all. She gazed across the square trying to locate her nemesis as well as searching for Ray Quinn. She found neither.

She forced herself to sip from the foamy brown and white mess resting on the top of the oversized bowl of a cup and winced at the bitterness. I could swim in there, she thought. Her mobile phone buzzed and bounced on the table in the throes of its vibration, before bursting into noisy life. Startled from her self-pity, Leanne grabbed it with both hands, anxious to prevent it crashing to the floor. With fear fumbling fingers she managed to press it to her ear.

"Not bad for an amateur," mocked the voice. "You've done well so far. Sit tight and wait."

From the comfort of the bench, and with the benefit of the low sun dazzling anybody looking directly at him from the coffee shop, Ray Quinn saw Leanne Lane emerge from the Conference Centre. Against the immense building she looked more vulnerable than ever and he was surprised by a rising urge to run over and gather her up safely. He saw her lunge at her phone and listen intently. He saw her puzzlement when she put it back on the table and sit back in her seat.

Minutes beforehand Frank had managed to find an empty seat along from the one recently vacated by Leanne. He'd been puzzled by her actions, but catching the bag she'd left behind, he suddenly realised what was going on. He stayed for the rest of the lecture, which was greeted at the end with tumultuous applause. As the clapping died away, people began gathering their belongings to leave. While appearing to scan the course brochure, Frank kept his eyes riveted on his target. As it was, he nearly missed the pick-up when it happened. A man shuffling along behind the row, a quick lean over the back of the seat and it was gone, but Frank had him: medium build, red hair, charcoal suit and a bag identical to at least fifty per cent of the other people in the room. Frank knew it was going to be tricky as two hundred delegates surged simultaneously towards the exits.

"Excuse me, excuse me," he repeated to anybody blocking his way, as he stumbled and skipped sideways between aisles to keep up. His quarry had moved off at a pace, but Frank stayed with him, ducking and diving his way through the crowd. Outside the lecture hall the task was much easier. Frank had expected him to make for the main entrance and the pick-up bays, to a waiting car, so he was surprised when he seemed to be heading in the opposite direction. He was making for the rear exit of the Conference Centre, going toward The Festival Hall and the canal, away from where Quinn was waiting. As he ran Frank put a call through to Quinn waiting outside.

"I've got him. Male, thirty-ish, five-eight, short, stocky, ginger hair, wearing a grey suit and white shirt."

"He's not coming my way," said Ray Quinn, "so where the hell is he off to?"

"I think he's going out the back way," said Frank, "towards the canal."

"Where the hell is he going?" shouted Ray Quinn at the phone, uncharacteristically agitated.

"The flat?" asked Frank.

It was certainly a possibility. They began moving to the other side of the building. But as Quinn ran, Frank's voice broke in again.

"We're going over the bridge towards the canal. Oh shit! You'd best get round here!"

"What?" asked Quinn.

Frank couldn't believe his eyes. Approaching the canal side, the man had suddenly broken into a run, at about the same time as Frank became aware of the background revving of a high-powered motor. It was over in no time as the man jumped into a motor-driven inflatable dinghy moored to the side of the canal. It roared away as the pursuers realised the hopelessness of their situation.

"Come on, I know where they're going," Quinn affirmed. "The canal doesn't go on forever. It gets close to the motorway, so they'll head north from there."

Quinn, in his hired car, and Frank, on his bike, gave chase. They swore in equal measure, but in the dense traffic Frank was able to take more risks and closed the gap sufficiently to spot a blue transit van parked on a side street. It was as close to the canal as any road could get and was about fifty yards from the motorway junction. It was the ideal spot. Weaving through the heavy traffic, progress was still painfully slow for Quinn and he had to rely on Frank to keep a close watch on the van.

Ray Quinn was painfully aware that he had left Leanne unguarded, but there was nothing he could do. He called and she told him everything. He took it all in quickly and told her to stay put, trying to transmit confidence and calm. He also told her not to worry, but he knew that had no effect. He was also mindful of Lomax and Billy, so he checked their status and was hugely relieved to find them untroubled. He asked whether they had seen Charlene and was not surprised by their negative response, because he was certain she was in the back of the transit van. He guessed they were either going to drop her unharmed at a motorway services or dump her suffering from a severe shortage of breath.

"She must be in the back of that van," said Quinn, talking to Frank on his mobile and sounding more confident than he really was.

"You think they'll keep her?" asked Frank.

"Or dump her off at a motorway services somewhere. What could be more natural? They can make it look as if they're dropping off a hitch-hiker, then blend back into the traffic."

They closed the gap as they talked. Just as the blue transit came into view Frank drove past it, round the corner and out of sight, made a three point turn, doubled back and pulled into a gap at the kerb-side. He called Quinn and confirmed his position. The driver of the Transit may have seen them, but Quinn doubted it. He was too busy watching for someone else.

With surprise on their side it should have been easy. Like many traumatic events things seemed to happen in slow motion. The getaway craft drew to a halt and, scrambling up the slipway, they made a run for the van. As the rear door was pulled to a close it began to pull away. Quinn's car screeched to a stop blocking the van. Frank was already on foot and had pinned two men to the floor. He was whispering in their ears, explaining reasons why they should remain perfectly still. One man didn't believe him, but was immediately convinced by the sight of his compatriot gasping for breath as Frank knelt on his windpipe, gradually exerting more pressure. Frank had indeed learned a great deal from his friend and mentor.

It was left to Ray Quinn to pursue the other escapee. He gave chase to the driver of the Transit, running along the towpath past soaring concrete pillars that shored up thousands of continuously flowing motorway vehicles. He sprinted into a dark and dank no-man's-land of concrete and scrubby wasteland that echoed to the deafening thunder of overhead traffic. The Transit driver ran behind a concrete pillar and sprinted into a tunnel. Quinn pursued him, his lungs burning, splatting through puddles that soaked his socks, pursuing his quarry into and out of the walkways that crossed and re-crossed the tarmac bound road maze as HGVs trundled along high bridges like a procession of lethargic snails.

For a while it looked as if Quinn would lose the runaway in the complex mass of tunnels and bridges, but following under a low, dark flyover he emerged to be confronted by a sheer forty-foot wall, the only way out via crudely hewn steps leading up to a slip road high above. Undeterred by the dead end, the driver was heaving himself upward already twenty feet from the ground. But this was Quinn's territory and launching himself at the wall, he ascended quickly and began to gain ground. He made a lunge for the man's ankle, but simultaneously the driver kicked out viciously, causing Quinn to momentarily lose his footing. For several seconds he flailed in mid-air while he struggled to regain a hold, before slithering down again over the jagged concrete, landing hard on the dirt at the bottom. The driver gave a triumphant leer back over his shoulder before vaulting over the crash barrier to freedom. Almost instantaneously, there came a prolonged, chilling screech followed by the smallest muffled thud and a cloud of bluish smoke billowed into the air. It was freedom short-lived. Quinn halted his pursuit before he could be seen and, gasping for breath, smiled. He turned up his collar, gathered himself and calmly walked away.

He returned to the Transit van, but Frank was waiting with more disappointment. All that had been found in the back of the van were some bags, clothing and empty fast-food cartons. Charlene wasn't there. Quinn asked about the two men who had succumbed to Frank's non too gentle questioning, but there was nothing to be gained from them.

"'What happened to the package?" asked Quinn, looking at Frank's two captives.

There was no response. This was largely because one of Frank's captives could not speak as his throat had been crushed beneath Frank's knee, and his partner seemed unwilling to part with any information.

"Oh please," said Ray Quinn. "Why am I having to repeat myself so much today? I won't ask again."

"You'd be well advised to answer his question," said Frank to the reluctant one, "my friend doesn't share my unending patience and forgiving nature, if you follow my meaning."

Realising the futility of silence he pointed at the grill of a storm drain in the gutter. "It's down there."

Ray Quinn rolled his eyes heavenwards and walked over to the drain. He peered down into a black abyss and his nasal passages were assaulted by the stench of sewage. He turned to the two captives and pointed to the man who had been so helpful.

"Your friend has suffered enough, I think. If we put him down there he'll only go and get an infection in his throat on top of his other troubles. It's down to you, I'm afraid. Be a good chap and retrieve our belongings, would you?"

The man stared at Quinn in stunned disbelief and remained rooted to the spot. Quinn lifted the drain cover with ease and moved swiftly across to him. He held the drain cover in one hand and gently laced the man's fingers through the grill bars, pinning them tightly with his other hand. His strength astonished his adversary.

"Now," said Quinn, "it's getting late and it's nearly time for my supper. I am a man of regular habits, and will have a meal in the next thirty minutes whatever happens. Either you'll be in that drain with the grill safely back in place while my friend and I enjoy our meal, or you will have found our items and possibly, just possibly, you could be breathing fresh air. It's really up to you. Don't forget though, you're making a decision for two people. It's called teamwork."

There was a husky intake of breath from the man with the damaged throat. He tried to free himself from Frank's grasp, but the attempt only brought more pain. Ray Quinn didn't wait for an answer. He pulled the man to the drain opening and swept his legs from under him. He was prostrate on the ground with his head over the hole before he knew what was happening.

"Oops," said Quinn, "that was clumsy. I apologise. Still, now you're there you may as well give it a go."

He unlocked his grip on the man's hand and pushed the grill away. "You can't get in carrying that, can you?" he said.

With one swift movement he tipped his quarry upside down and, holding him only by his ankles, lowered him headfirst downwards.

"I think you'll have to use your hands; you surely can't see anything can you?" asked Quinn, lowering the man a touch further so that the top of his head was washed by the foul waters. "Don't worry, I've got you. You can rely on me."

The unfortunate man stretched out his arms and began to search frantically for the bag that he himself had thrown there.

"You know," mused Quinn to Frank, "I'll have a bet with you that it was my friend down there who is the litterbug. It's only fair that he should pick up his own rubbish, don't you think?"

The man being held by Frank nodded vigorously, hoping his agreement would spare him. Frank merely smiled at Quinn's dark humour, knowing what the outcome would be. They were interrupted by the upside down man wriggling madly, trying to bend backwards to pass his find up to Quinn. Letting go with one hand, Quinn grabbed the bag and peered inside. He smiled when he saw the findings from the library and, equally important, the cash bundled neatly in its bank bindings. Remarkably everything was dry, thanks to having been carefully wrapped in plastic bags and tied tightly.

"That's it. Well done that man!" he said. "It must have got snagged on something, otherwise it would be miles away by now. Are you sure that's everything?"

The man waved his arms to indicate there was no more to be found.

"Perhaps you should make sure. I'd hate for you have to do it all over again," said Quinn as he released his grip and the man plunged out of sight. He said nothing as he calmly picked up the grill and stamped it back into place over the hole. He looked at the remaining captive. "You will notice that you've escaped the same fate as your friend. I didn't think you'd quite fit through the hole, so you'll have to accept our hospitality for a while longer."

The man made no sound as he collapsed in Frank's arms.

"Take him back to the flat," said Quinn to Frank. "Clean him up, give him something to eat and drink. Show him we're not animals. He needs to be convinced that working for Jack Noble is not a good lifestyle choice. I'll leave that bit to you. You'll have to take the car and I'll use your bike. Oh, by the way. There's something in the boot that needs special care. I'd like you to take personal charge of it until I get there. I'd better get a move on and retrieve Leanne. Hopefully, she'll still be sitting in the coffee shop awaiting instructions."

-20-

Leanne finished her third cup and was awash with coffee. She needed to deal with its effects, but was afraid to leave her seat in case that would be the very time something happened. It's well known that women can resist the urge to empty their bladders for far longer than men, but just as she decided to give up the unequal fight Ray Quinn walked into view. He had returned to his bench across the square and waited there for a full fifteen minutes, making sure that nobody else was taking an interest in Leanne. He watched as she gazed at an information system which was on a loop around the top of a building rather like the Stock Exchange issuing the latest share prices and news. He glanced at it from time to time and was vaguely amused. It had become well known for its out of the ordinary content. Today someone with a sense of humour had placed oddball definitions to spread smiles across the square and both Quinn and Leanne followed the moving text from their separate positions.

'ADULT: a person who has stopped growing at both ends and is now growing in the middle......CHICKENS: the only animals you eat before they are born and after they are dead...COMMITTEE: a body that keeps minutes and wastes hours.....DUST: mud with the juice squeezed out.......EGOTIST: someone who is usually me-deep in conversation.....HANDKERCHIEF: cold storage.........INFLATION......cutting money in half without damaging the paper......RAISIN: a grape with sunburn......SECRET: something you tell to one person at a time......SKELETON.....a bunch of bones with the person scraped off......TOOTHACHE: the pain that drives you to extraction.......TOMORROW: one of the greatest labour saving devices of today.....YAWN: an honest opinion openly expressed.....WRINKLES: something other people have, similar to my character lines.'

The loop was on its umpteenth repetition, before he made his approach.

"Is this seat taken?" he asked politely for the benefit of other ears.

"No, please feel free," replied Leanne matching his courtesy.

Quinn sat opposite Leanne Lane, placed his hands together on the table and gave her his best winning smile. Anybody watching the performance would assume they were meeting for the first time, having been matched by an online dating agency, and would be going for a meal somewhere in town.

"Coffee?" enquired Quinn.

"No thanks," she replied. "I've had more than enough already. In fact I really have to pay a visit. I've been stuck here in case I missed something or somebody. They told me to wait here and not to move."

"They won't be contacting you," Quinn assured her. "Things have moved on a bit. I'll wait here while you do what comes naturally."

Leanne breathed a sigh of relief and hurried away into the depths of the coffee shop. Quinn watched her all the way until she disappeared through the appropriate door. His eyes made another sweep looking out for any sign of interest in Leanne or himself. He dug into his trouser pocket and extricated a scrap of paper upon which he had written the number of a taxi company and a driver's licence number. He used his mobile to request that driver in particular. He was told it would take ten minutes for him to get there, but Quinn insisted he wanted that driver and said he was happy to wait. He looked around again and, satisfied that all was well, he stood up as Leanne returned. He didn't want her to sit again.

"We need to get back to the flat," he said. "Unfortunately, I came here by bike and I haven't got a spare helmet, so you'll have to use a taxi. He's on his way now. Don't worry, I'll be right behind. Nothing will happen."

Leanne instantly remembered an earlier bike ride and was thankful not to have to repeat it. Quinn spotted her relief. He laughed and she couldn't help laughing too. The taxi appeared and Quinn ushered Leanne inside. As she was in the process of settling into taking her seat, Quinn arrived behind her. Puzzled, she gave him a quizzical look. He responded by putting his forefinger to his lips. He slid the vanity glass across and addressed the driver.

"Hello," he said," you may not remember me, but you made an impression on me the last time we met." He put his face closer to the opening to allow the driver a closer look. "Remember now? I thought so," he said as the driver's eyes betrayed him. "I asked for you specifically as I thought I'd give you the opportunity to make amends. I need you to take me to the train station, so that I may collect my bike. Then we need to get this good lady home. I'll follow on the bike. Seeing as you tried to overcharge me before, and today's journey is not all that far, let's agree that there will be no charge. If all goes well, that will be the end of the matter. I'm sure you wouldn't want any further complications, would you?" Quinn treated the man to a meaningful smile and the one-sided debate was over.

Ray Quinn helped Leanne exit the taxi. He turned his attention to the driver, who was badly shaken by the constant looming presence of the bike and the impenetrable helmet in his rear view mirror.

"Thank you," he said pleasantly. "Now I'll be able to recommend you to my friends. Don't worry they pay better than me!"

Leanne and Quinn watched as the driver scuttled away as quickly as his cab and its diesel engine's tapping rattle, would allow.

They walked into the flat to be greeted with handshakes and hugs by Lomax and Billy. Frank was standing in the corner of the living room, close to a window.

"Where's our throaty friend?" enquired Quinn.

"Resting," replied Frank. "He's had a rather traumatic time, I'm afraid. He only wanted to sleep when we got back here, but you asked me to talk to him about his lifestyle. I'm afraid he was somewhat reticent at first but I believe he now sees the error of his ways."

John Lomax giggled quietly.

"Why is it," he asked his friend Ray Quinn," that anybody who is in your company for a period of time becomes almost a clone?"

"No idea," answered Quinn with a grin, "it must be a gift."

"I'm hungry," moaned Billy, "anybody fancy ordering a Chinese?"

"Good idea," said Lomax and wrote down everyone's wishes. "What about our resting friend?"

"Leave him, "said Frank. "I don't think he's hungry right now. Anyway, we'll only have to blitz it and feed him through a straw. Too much trouble for my liking."

Nobody disagreed and Billy phoned the order through. They then turned their attention to analysis and planning.

"So," Quinn began, "we've now got plenty of money. You have still got it Frank," he asked.

"Of course," replied Frank with a smile. "Why doubt it?"

"I gave my word to Noble that he'd get his other half within seven days," said Quinn. I don't want to break my promise so if we have to pay John's debt to Jack Noble we'll do so using his own cash. At least we haven't lost anything. In fact we're very much in profit. I asked Billy to come here to help get money for John and we've done that. I did not bank on Charlene becoming involved."

The last comment was a direct reference to his directive that Billy should come alone. Billy reddened at the overt criticism, but Quinn ignored his discomfort and continued.

"I didn't want that and hadn't planned for it, but we now have no choice. It was the first item on our list when we last went through all this and now it's become top priority. We must find her as soon as possible. The longer she's out there, the more danger she's in. Apart from that, all the other things we identified have still to be covered. To reiterate: Apart from finding Charlene, we need to settle Jack Noble, return Billy and Charlene to Australia and we need to sort out John and Leanne's situation."

Ray Quinn did not mention that his own future was inextricably linked to the whole issue, but he had already started thinking about it. The intercom buzzed as the food arrived. Billy collected it at the entrance. Once it had been set out on the table plates were put in front of each of them.

"I can't remember what I ordered," said Leanne.

"Doesn't matter," said Lomax, "let's all just dig in and share. It's no time for niceties."

Silence descended as five hungry people made short work of their tasty food. Five brains worked overtime as they ate, but nobody seemed to want to be first to speak. Eventually, as the last of the meal was consumed, Quinn posed the question.

"Any ideas? I know what I think we should do, but I'd like to hear what you all have to say."

Nobody spoke. There was a tangible reluctance to appear stupid.

"I think I can help," offered Frank, looking at the expectant faces around the table. "Our resting friend was keen to share his burden, so I know where we can find Charlene. Obviously there is a chance that he may have told me lies, but I really don't think so. By the end of our conversation he was thankful to have been able to clear his conscience. I thanked him for his assistance, but made no promises as to his future."

"How did you manage it?" asked Billy.

"You should know better than to ask," Frank reprimanded him, "but if you must know I used my very limited artistic skills to draw a simple sketch of a drain cover being held by a matchstick man and another man looking down into a hole in the ground. I think he got the message."

"Inventive," said an impressed Ray Quinn. His friend Frank was showing promise.

"What on earth is that all about?" asked Leanne at the same time as Billy asked "what does that mean?

"None of your business," said Ray Quinn with authority.

-21-

Apart from an ominous creaking and whirring of the lift mechanism, the trio descended to the basement floor in silence while Quinn gave Leanne and Billy time and space to assimilate what they'd been told. Frank was exercising some discretion too. He had wanted to accompany them, but had finally agreed to remain at the flat and look after John Lomax and keep the resting man under control.

Frank had passed on the information that Charlene had been left by some of Jack Noble's accomplices in a room in the basement of the apartment building. He told Quinn that she had apparently been drugged to the extent that, to an untrained eye, she appeared dead and it had been made to look like suicide. Quinn decided not to pass the information to the others because he knew suicide threw up all kinds of powerful and often unwanted emotions. He also reasoned that they would act more effectively if their reactions were genuine. Quinn was the first to think of the solution and the others helped complete the minor details. It was entirely possible that they were walking into a trap, but Frank had been adamant that he believed there would be no opposition.

The first thing they noticed as they entered the room was that it was icily cold. The other details made themselves apparent thereafter. It reminded Ray Quinn of the room from which he had rescued Billy after his assignation with the brunette and Quinn realised that it was meant to. They were being given a highly personal message. There was a woman, curled into the foetal position, with unblinking staring eyes and there was an unmoving man on the floor with a needle hanging from his forearm. There were also newspaper cuttings with highlighted advertisements for personal escort services. A pro would have cleaned up, but whoever had set up this tableau knew what he wanted them to find. Quinn knew it was becoming increasingly commonplace for some higher class call girls to supply, and if that was the case it would explain why everything had been left just so. Quinn was unsure of the identity of the unblinking woman, but Billy knew as soon as he set eyes upon her. He was completely overcome with guilt and fear and was rooted to the spot. Quinn looked at Leanne, who was taking in the scene and hiding her reaction very well. Quinn knew better than to make any comments at that stage, because death is much like life in that everybody handles it in his or her own unique way. Shock can do funny things to people and Quinn bided his time. He wanted Billy to be gradually overtaken by thoughts of atonement and then revenge.   The more genuine those feelings were, the better it would be.

"Are you alright?" he asked Leanne. She was clearly shocked, as Quinn would have expected, but still far from being distressed. Instead, she appeared more puzzled and detached as if presented with a conundrum.

"Are you all right?" he repeated.

"Yes." With a brief nod of thanks, she awkwardly moved close, as if seeking reassurance. I just can't believe it."

Ray Quinn looked at her and her eyes looked directly into his, steady and unblinking. There was no avoidance, but no trace of any tears either.

She read his thoughts. "You must think I'm hard." It wasn't an apology and Quinn only shrugged.

"Everyone reacts differently in these situations," he said. "You'll probably cry your eyes out when we get back."

Leanne smiled weakly. "That's tactful of you,' she said. "But I don't think so. If I do, it will be for Billy," she whispered softly, hoping her son hadn't heard the exchange.

"I don't understand," Billy's voice was shaky and uncertain. "Charlene.....she's never used drugs. What's happening?"

"People change," said Leanne showing little compassion. "Sometimes pretty dramatically."

"Not in these few days!" said Billy, his eyes welling with tears.

"It can happen," continued Leanne, choosing to ignore the growing rift between mother and son which was becoming increasingly painful for both of them.

"'No!" The anger flared from Billy as he turned to face his mother, adopting a threatening posture.

The silence stretched to breaking point as each stood their ground.

Quinn spoke sharply, "we haven't got time for this! You can sort it out later. We need to get Charlene away from here now."

His words cut into each of them

"Is she going to be alright?" asked Billy, gazing with love and tenderness at her small and fragile body.

"I don't know," replied Quinn, "but we can't deal with it here. She's alive but she needs all sorts of help, and I don't just mean the medical variety."

"What on earth do you mean?" Billy reacted swiftly in her defence. "She's a perfectly normal, beautiful woman."

"And head butting people is a normal part of her behaviour, is it?" Quinn persisted. "We found her hiding in a cupboard under the stairs and when we let her out, she went crazy and John's nose got in her way."

Billy shook his head in disbelief at Ray Quinn's lack of understanding.

"Look," continued Quinn patiently, "I've had plenty of experience with users, you don't have to pretend to me and Frank's also had first- hand experience of it; he can straighten her out. I'd trust him with my life and you can too. He'll get her off the stuff, but it won't be easy. First, though we need to move. Don't touch anything if you can help it."

"She is not a user," Billy persisted, "she was just frightened. She's terrified of the dark and enclosed spaces. When that door was opened she just panicked and came flying out. Check her over for yourself; you won't find any tracks on her arms, I promise you."

Ray Quinn was unused to being proved wrong and didn't quite know how to react. "I'm sorry," he whispered, "it appears I jumped to the wrong conclusion. Let's get her back to the flat, there's nothing we can do here."

"What about the newspaper cuttings" asked Leanne.

"Oh, I think we'll leave those here. I don't think Charlene needs to see them, do you Billy?" said Quinn.

Billy nodded his head in agreement and smiled his silent thanks to Ray Quinn. He bent down and tenderly gathered Charlene, still in her foetal position, into his arms. He straightened his back and turned to follow Leanne. Ray Quinn watched and saw the love in the young man's eyes as he looked at Charlene's pale face.

The mood for their reunion at the flat was not celebratory and an uneasy quiet prevailed. Charlene had not woken from her drug induced stupor and Billy was at the bedside, desperately worried. She was breathing, but it was shallow, rapid and uneven and he noticed that she was sweating profusely. Leanne sat beside Lomax in the living room, holding his hand as they whispered in tones too soft for the others to hear. Frank and Quinn parked themselves in the kitchen, hands gripped around mugs of coffee, recognising that people needed space and time to recover. The resting man was still resting and would do so for quite some time to come. Frank had put him through an ordeal the like of which he had never before experienced or witnessed. It had been the only way to extract the vital information required to affect Charlene's rescue.

"He'll survive, I expect," said Frank, although Quinn noted that he didn't sound entirely convinced.

"It doesn't matter either way," responded Quinn. "He's no more use to us." His voice trailed off as he lapsed into thoughtful silence. "On the other hand, we could send him back to Noble as a message."

"That's risky, Ray," said Frank. "He'll lead Noble here."

Their deliberations were interrupted by Billy as he walked slowly into the kitchen.

"How is she?" asked Frank.

"Asleep," replied Billy, despair etched into his face.

"She's not asleep, she's unconscious," said Frank. "It looks like she's been given cocaine. Do you know much about it?"

"No!" Billy was startled at the mere suggestion.

"I didn't mean have you taken it, Billy, I meant do you know much about the drug itself and what it can do?"

"The answer's still no," replied Billy, trying to settle his inner turmoil.

"Then sit down and I'll educate you. Cocaine is a stimulant manufactured from leaves taken off the coca plant. There are specific cocaine overdose symptoms that should be watched for to recognize an overdose at its earliest stage. By catching the overdose as early as possible and getting immediate treatment, the user has a better chance of avoiding serious injury. When ingested, it increases alertness, causes euphoria and leads to general feelings of well-being. We haven't seen that in Charlene, though. Actual use and overdose can have different signs. Have you noticed dilated pupils, high energy levels, greatly increased activity, excitability or enthusiastic speech? The time these things last depends on how the cocaine has been taken. Obviously smoking or injecting makes it happen faster so the effects last for a shorter time. It can be difficult to spot. Perhaps you can think of times when she's been like that." Frank paused to allow Billy the opportunity to think and reply.

"I haven't seen any of the things you've described," said Billy.

"I have," said John Lomax, who had come into the kitchen unnoticed. "She was very excitable when I opened that cupboard door and she smashed me on the nose." He ran his fingers lightly over his misshapen nose and heavily bruised cheeks.

"I've explained that," countered Billy. "She's scared to death of closed in spaces and the dark. It was no wonder she bolted."

"It suits you," grinned Ray Quinn, trying to lease the tension. "It's given your face character, don't you think, Leanne?"

"Wonderful improvement," she said with all the sarcasm she could muster.

"So, let's move on," said Frank. "An overdose from cocaine use can have significant effects. The symptoms are easily recognizable. The normal side effects of the drug's use include a rise in the user's body temperature, heart rate and blood pressure. While these effects are rarely in the dangerous range for those in good health, they can be dangerous to those who have previous conditions, such as high blood pressure or a heart condition. For those people, an overdose can lead to abdominal pain and nausea, seizures, heart attack, stroke or respiratory failure. Cocaine overdose symptoms are both physical and psychological. They include nausea, vomiting, tremors, irregular breathing, increased temperature and heart rate, chest pains seizures, anxiety, agitation, paranoia, panic, hallucination, and delirium. Is that enough education for one day?" he asked with a smile.

"Ok, so you know what to look for in a user and how to recognise an overdose, though I hate to imagine where you came by all this information," said Leanne.

Ray Quinn and Frank exchanged a rapid and meaningful glance.

"That doesn't matter, does it? said Frank. "The important thing for us now, and of course Charlene, is what to do about it all." He didn't wait for a response. "Normally, she should be taken to hospital straight away, but I don't suppose that's an option, so we'll have to treat her as a doctor would and the sooner the better. A doctor would treat cocaine overdose as a poisoning, but unlike some poisons, there is no antidote. She must be constantly monitored. As she's unconscious she needs ventilation and she might need saline for hydration. If she's burning hot, we might have to sedate her and put her in an ice bath. There is a risk her heart may stop, but we'll deal with that then. With luck she should gradually return to normal. It really all depends on how much of an overdose she has been given. And there, children, endeth the lesson."

The kitchen was silent as each digested the information.

"Can you deal with all that?" asked Billy, fearful now.

"Yes," replied Frank, "but I'll need your help. John, I've made a list of things I need. Would you slip out and get them from the nearest chemist?"

"Of course," said Lomax, pleased to be given something practical to do.

"I'll come with you," said Leanne.

"No," Quinn said sharply. "I don't want more than one person out at a time. Look how difficult it's been to get us all together here. Be careful, John."

"Remember what your mother told you; don't stop and talk to strangers." Leanne's sarcasm had not abated.

"Right," said Quinn, "John, you fetch the stuff that Frank and Billy need, and I'll deal with our resident resting man. I may need some help with that, so I'll wait until you get back, John, and then the three of us can sort it out. Oh, and I'm going to have to talk to Charlene."

"I'm sorry to have to disappoint you, Ray, but she won't be making any sense for a quite a while," said Frank.

"I'll still need to talk to her as soon as possible," said Quinn with authority.

Leanne watched Lomax leave and returned her attention to Quinn.

"You haven't told us what you intend to do with our resting friend," said Leanne.

"That's because I hadn't decided until now. I believe we should hide him away. Jack Noble will be missing him," mused Quinn. "Come on Leanne, you can help me. We might as well make use of the time until John gets back."

The resting man was bundled up and shoved unceremoniously onto the back seat of the BMW. He didn't respond in any way because he was so heavily drugged that he was lucky to be alive. They drove for over half an hour through darkening lanes until they reached the electric gates of an expensive looking property on the outskirts of the city. The plaque on the gate post bore the legend 'Priory Place – No cold callers.' Ray Quinn smiled at the irony.

"How do you know this is the right place?" enquired Leanne.

"Because Frank told me. It seems our friend on the back seat was very keen to help as much as he could and Frank promised him home comforts in return. This will be his home for a while. He won't remember anything, though, after what Frank's given him."

He stopped the car and switched off the engine. He quietly opened the door and stepped out onto the tarmac surface. He had made sure they had halted just out of the range of motion sensor lights or cameras, but nevertheless told Leanne to stay in the car and keep watch. He dragged the inert body out and placed the resting man sitting upright, leaning on a fence. He made sure he was still breathing and slipped back behind the wheel. Satisfied, he eased the car away and accelerated only when they were a good distance from the gates. Leanne did not notice Quinn slip an envelope into the man's pocket, nor did she notice the resting man being lifted by two members of staff and taken inside.

-22-

"She's awake!" shouted Billy, unable to hide his relief.

Frank leapt up and sprinted to Charlene. "Don't leave her alone," he shouted as he went past Billy. "This is going to be difficult for her."

Nobody knew how accurate those words were going to be. Frank and Billy tended to her every need for many days, but, although she was recovering in the physical sense, her mental state proved an intractable problem. Eventually, after much soul searching, it was agreed that she needed specialist care. Charlene's health was the key for all of them. Billy couldn't be settled without her; their two year old son needed her; Leanne and John could not be free to live the rest of their lives unless Billy and Charlene were sorted out as well as Jack Noble. For Quinn and Frank it all represented unfinished business.

It was decided that Charlene should be nursed at Priory Place. It was a convenient arrangement because they could also keep a watchful eye on the resting man at the same time. Quinn left strict instructions that the two new inmates must never meet nor even set eyes on each other.

Over the course of the next month a pattern of visiting became established. Leanne, Lomax and Billy visited Charlene individually and occasionally in pairs, whilst Quinn and Frank went to see the resting man. The pattern changed occasionally and so it was that Quinn and Leanne came to be on visiting duty together.

Priory Place was Monday morning busy when a security guard let Quinn and Leanne in with a smile and a pleasantry.

"That resting man isn't resting anymore," said the guard." He's been creating havoc."

"Doing what?" asked Leanne.

"Trying to crack his head open on the walls, mainly. We've put him in a safety room for now. Through here."

Moving swiftly on he led the way through a maze of brightly lit corridors, until they reached a door, which he pushed open, standing aside to allow them in. The room itself was empty but the entire width of the end wall was panelled with glass and on the other side was the Resting Man.

"We really must find him a name," said Quinn, as much to himself as to Leanne or the guard. "We'll come back to him later," he said. "We'd like to see Charlene now."

The sight of Charlene shocked them both. Clad in a dressing gown, she paced restlessly around the perimeter of the room, stopping now and then at some random spot to spread the fingers of both hands on the wall, laying her cheek in between, as if listening for something on the other side. Her wild, agitated appearance emphasised her distressed state, but even so Quinn was struck by underlying fragility and beauty. The guard eased back to allow a doctor to step alongside them.

"She's in the agitated phase," he announced.

"How long will it last?" asked Leanne.

"We can't tell," said the doctor gently. "It varies from case to case. Thankfully, I think we can say there should be no long term damage."

"Billy will be pleased," reflected Leanne.

"I think it would help speed her recovery if she could be surrounded by people and things she loves," offered the doctor.

"That sounds the right kind of thing,' Leanne agreed. "We'll bring some stuff in tomorrow."

"She keeps asking for Billy," said the doctor.

"He'll be in tomorrow as well," said Quinn, "I'll make sure he comes."

"You do know that she's here voluntarily," the doctor said. "Nobody can legally stop her leaving, although we would try to dissuade her obviously."

"Yes, we know," replied Leanne.

"Do you think it could help if Billy took her out for a while?" he asked. He was getting the impression that the doctor was subtly suggesting a change.

"I don't think it will do any harm," Mr Quinn.

"Good, then that's what we'll do. Billy and I will pick her up tomorrow morning, say about ten?"

"That will be fine," replied the doctor, obviously pleased that he was dealing with a man who recognised and appreciated his subtlety. He was also pleased with the fact that he had not been asked to give his name.

Billy was overjoyed by the news that it was time to take Charlene out, if only for a little while, but Quinn tempered his joy with words of caution when they reached the car.

"Listen, Billy, I know you'll be glad to have Charlene back with you, but I'm not doing this just for that reason. You do realise that the only way to sort out this whole sorry mess is to use her to get to Jack Noble, don't you? He won't let it go, Billy. We, no you actually, owe John Lomax for everything he's done. Come to think of it you also owe me, but I'm not going to worry about that. Also, your mother wants to see you settled and happy and she knows Charlene's the one for you. You cannot afford to make a mess of this, Billy."

"I know," replied Billy, finding it difficult to look Ray Quinn in the eye.

"How well do you know me?" asked Quinn.

"Enough to know I can trust you," replied Billy.

"How well do you know John Lomax?"

"Enough to know I can trust him as well," said Billy, puzzled by the questioning.

"Last question; how well do you know your mother?" asked Quinn.

"I love her," said Billy.

"That's not what I asked," said Quinn quietly.

"I know," replied Billy, but I don't think I can answer your question.

"Good. That's an honest answer. I can work with that."

"Can you really sort all this out, Ray?" asked Billy.

"I can't," said Quinn, but we can. That's what I'm getting at. We must all trust each other. It's going to get worse before it gets better. There will be times in the next few days when we'll all be tested to the limit, and doubts will creep in. I'm not going to be very pleasant, but remember it's for a reason. You'll see me do things and say things that may repulse you. I'll push each one of you to the edge, including Charlene, and success depends on how you deal with it. If you don't think you can do this, you'd better say so now."

"I don't understand," said Billy.

"You don't need to know all the details," said Quinn. "The most important thing you will need to hang onto is the fact that Charlene loves you. She followed you all the way from Australia and is in a real mess now. If you let her down now, you'll never see your little boy again and she may never recover either."

"What about mother?" asked Billy. "What do I do about her?"

"Nothing. You don't need to do anything. What will be, will be. She will be sorted out as things progress. You'll have to use up some of your trust in me with that one."

"Have you had this conversation with the others?" asked Billy.

Ray Quinn smiled. "No, and before you ask, I have my reasons. Suffice it to say that they'll understand eventually."

When they returned the following morning Charlene was dressed and ready to go. She flung her arms round Billy's neck and wouldn't let go until he eventually prised her fingers free one by one. He smiled and laughed with her, as he took her by the hand and they hurried out of Priory Place.

Ray Quinn watched it all with a warm glow, but did not let it continue for long. He had already decided that the action would begin today.

"Be careful, Billy" he said, "remember John Lomax's re-arranged nose." He was deliberately beginning to apply pressure to them both, because he wanted to test their reactions.

Billy shot him an appalled look, but Charlene didn't even seem to notice.

"I think we should take her back to the house?" said Quinn.

"Not the flat?" asked Billy.

"No. I said the house. You know, the one that rents rooms by the hour. I think it might be worth a try," continued Quinn.

Quinn drove while Billy and Charlene sat in the back. He had already taken the precaution of setting the child locks to the rear doors. There was no conversation as he drove, but he kept glancing in the rear view mirror and was pleased to note that they were holding hands. He was taking them back to the room in which Charlene had been locked in an under stair cupboard. He was keen to asses her reaction. He hoped they would learn something.

As he drew up in front of the building Charlene became agitated. She withdrew her hand from Billy's grip and reached towards the window. She tested the door handle and began to panic when it wouldn't work.

"She thinks we're going to shut her in the cupboard again. We've brought her back here too soon. This is too frightening for her," said Billy.

"Shut up, Billy," rasped Quinn.

He was pleased to see that Charlene immediately cupped her hands protectively around Billy's face as the shock of Quinn's reprimand hit him.

"Terrific," commented Quinn, pondering on his next move. He didn't want to upset Charlene further and he decided to leave. He took a last look around and spotted the front door of the adjacent house open. A woman emerged, carrying a small fluffy canine, and stepped delicately around the piles of sand and bricks.

"Hold on." Seeing an opportunity Quinn jumped out of the car and introduced himself over the low hedge. The woman squinted at him through bottle-end glasses, trying to look over his shoulder towards the car.

"Have you got Charlene in there? I thought so."

"And you are ... ?" he asked.

"I live next door," she replied evasively.

Quinn decided not to pursue that point. Her name wasn't important and she no doubt had her reasons. Perhaps in return she wouldn't ask his name.

She shook her head sadly. "I can't believe a thing like that could happen round here."

Quinn thought to himself that news certainly travelled fast. "Did you notice anything out of the ordinary?" he asked.

"No . .I've had the workmen here working on the drive. This job should have been finished in three days, but you know what it's like. They start one thing and then there's a problem. Five days it's been going on and it's still not done."

"Did you know the man or the woman?" Quinn cut in.

"Not really, no. We only moved in two years ago in February. The man seemed to live there all the time, but we hardly ever saw him. He had lots of girls visit him, though. We were out here when that one came. I told her we lived next door and asked her name. That's how I know she's called Charlene. She seemed different to the others; you know, nicer, if you know what I mean."

"I understand perfectly," said Ray Quinn, smiling at her.

"I assumed it was just another girl, but I hoped for his sake it was more than that," the woman continued. "You don't like to be nosy, do you?"

Quinn thought that took a stretch of his imagination.

"'We were just pleased to see that he had found a nicer young lady. The others had skirts up to their embarrassment, but she was different."

Quinn was surprised by her clever use of language.

She went on. "He seemed such a decent man."

Quinn thought that even more of a stretch of the imagination, but he decided not to disillusion the woman. He also decided not to ask questions about the man. He already knew enough about him.

"But if I can be of any more help, officer.." the woman was still talking as he turned to leave.

After what he'd just heard, he doubted that she could, but he politely nodded thanks anyway, deciding not to inform her he was not from the police. He went back to the car, mulling over the new information.

"Don't worry, Charlene," he said as he sat down, "you don't need to go back in there."

Charlene broke down and wept bitterly. She clung on to Billy for all she was worth and her stuttering and muffled words came through her tears, as she pressed her face into Billy's chest.

"Thank you, thank you, thank you."

-23-

"Now we need to find Jack Noble," announced Ray Quinn the following morning over breakfast. We've rattled his cage, but he doesn't seem to want to put in an appearance. Wherever he is, we need to find him. I'll need to go back to our resting friend at Priory Place and see if he can help."

Ray Quinn also had other plans. He decided that it was time for Billy to step up to the mark. If Billy and Charlene were to have a future, then Billy would have to fight for it. He was not going to lay it on a plate for him. He had also decided to keep a much closer eye on Leanne. Her flirtatious behaviour had not gone unnoticed and he needed to nip it in the bud. John Lomax was owed that at the very least. He was ensuring he maintained the momentum. He wanted all concerned, friend and foe, to be off balance. He had not discussed his intentions with Frank, but he knew he would realise what was happening and react accordingly. He hoped Lomax would also understand.

"I think the best thing is to go back to the flat and pick up your mother, Billy. Charlene needs a woman with her at the moment and I need you to do something for me."

He drove back to the flat with the car in silence. Charlene was hanging on to Billy, who was at a loss as to what Ray Quinn was up to now. He brought the car to a halt, but kept the engine running.

"Say your goodbyes, Billy, then go inside and fetch your mother. Tell her to bring her overnight bag. Don't worry Charlene, I'll look after you, I just need Billy to do something for me."

"But, I don't understand. Charlene needs me with her. What's going on?" pleaded Billy.

"Don't ask questions, we haven't the time," asserted Quinn, turning to face Billy in the rear seat.

Billy kissed Charlene tenderly, gave her a reassuring hug and walked into the flat. He had been given no choice; no leeway. Ray Quinn in this mood was not a man it was worthwhile challenging. He just had to trust him.

Leanne appeared a short while later, carrying a small bag. She opened the front passenger side door.

"No, you sit in the back with Charlene," said Quinn. "She needs you now."

Leanne slammed the door with more than the necessary force and Charlene jumped with shock. Quinn looked in the rear view mirror and noted that Leanne was sitting as far apart from Charlene as possible and sulking like an adolescent schoolgirl. She had obviously been fooled into thinking the need for her overnight bag was the result of her advances to Quinn. She had fallen at the first fence and she would have to prove herself more and more as time went on if Ray Quinn was to be able to leave his friend John Lomax in her tender care. It amused him to think that she would be tested to the limit before long.

"All buckled up?" he asked.

"Yes," replied Charlene. Leanne did not respond.

Quinn drove without hurry to Priory Place. When they arrived he courteously opened the back doors for the two women to slide out. Leanne's bag remained in the foot well of the front seat, but she didn't notice the only bag he was carrying was Charlene's. They spent a good hour settling Charlene back into her room at Priory Place and, although Quinn was anxious to move on, he knew it was time well spent. His resources were stretched and he needed Charlene to feel safe so that he did not have to keep worrying about her as he drove things forward.

"It's time we went," announced Quinn, "Leanne and I need to chase something up. You'll be fine here, Charlene. I'll ask the doctor to look in on you shortly."

He gave her a hug in what was, for him, an unusual display of affection. Leanne merely smiled at her and raised her hand in half-hearted farewell.

"I need to look in on our resting man," announced Quinn.

With Leanne in tow, he sought and found the doctor.

"How's our resting man?" asked Quinn.

"Much the same," the doctor replied. "He's asleep at the moment and I'd like him to stay that way, if you don't mind. If you need to talk to him, perhaps you could come back tomorrow."

"That's fine." Quinn was in no hurry; tomorrow would do.

Leanne trailed behind like an obedient puppy.

"Am I allowed in the front now?" she asked, the question dripping with sarcasm.

"Naturally," he said, "why not?" He replied, ignoring the acid.

"What now?" she asked.

It was obvious to Quinn what she wanted and, smiling inwardly, he restricted himself to a sigh. He looked at the front of Priory Place and noticed that it was already in darkness. The only illumination was provided by the lights of the drive.

The doctor turned out the light and watched them leave, peeping round the edge of drawn curtains. He smiled, turned and made his way to the room where the resting man was far from asleep.

-24-

"I need a drink," said Quinn. "You?"

Oh yes," she said.

They found themselves a quiet corner in a nearby bar and after fifteen minutes of meaningless chatter, their drinks sat untouched on the table in front of them.

"Ray, I am sorry," Leanne finally got to the point. "It's just that there is a magnetism about you that I can't ignore. You must have noticed women being attracted to you."

"I can't say I have," replied Quinn, inwardly pleased by the news. "But, I can't let this go any further. John is my friend and I just couldn't do it to him. More importantly, I'm married and intend to stay that way."

"She's a very lucky woman," commented Leanne. "If I were her, I wouldn't let you out of my sight."

"She knows she can trust me," Quinn responded. "If I were John Lomax I wouldn't let you out of my sight either, because he obviously shouldn't trust you."

"I'll behave, don't worry. I know he loves me and I'd have too much to lose."

Ray Quinn decided to leave it there. If Leanne let herself and Lomax down again, she would only have herself to blame. Nevertheless, he promised himself that he would discuss the matter with his friend at the earliest opportunity.

"I'm hungry. Shall we eat here? It seems as good a place as any."

"Fine," she replied, "it will do us good to do something normal."

They ate and chatted for a good half an hour and the atmosphere between them became less charged as Quinn worked to put Leanne back into a happier place. They had just begun coffee when Quinn's mobile announced itself.

"What now?" he asked. "For two pins I'd throw this thing in the river. They've taken over our lives. Hello," he barked irritably.

"Ray, sorry to disturb you. It's Frank."

"Trouble?" asked Quinn, glancing at Leanne simultaneously. "Hang on, I'll turn the volume up. Whatever it is, Leanne should hear it as well."

"Are you sure?" asked Frank.

"Definitely," asserted Quinn.

Frank understood perfectly. "I'm at the flat with John. Billy's disappeared. We've looked all over but he's vanished into thin air. I was getting some sleep when John burst in and told me Billy is nowhere to be seen. Is he with you?"

Quinn gave Leanne a meaningful glance and her heart pumped. "No," he said. "I specifically told him to stay there until I got back. Why on earth does he insist on disappearing? It's getting an annoying habit."

"Hang on Ray, John's just found a note. It's not Billy's writing. I'll read it to you. Oh, it's hard to read, the writing's terrible."

Leanne's curiosity knew no bounds as she took it all in.

"Don't bother, Frank. Just send it to my phone now. Is John alright?"

"Yes, he's fine. I'm sending it now. I'll hang on here in case Billy comes back."

"Good. Yes, I've got it. Thanks. Wait a minute." Quinn's lips moved as he read silently from his phone. "Frank, you need to batten down the hatches. Lock all doors, shut every window. Neither of you must leave the flat. Be with John all the time. Do not let him out of your sight. Sleep in the same room if you have to. The resting man's out of Priory Place and he's gone after Billy. I don't give much for his chances without help. Jack Noble's behind this, I bet. He's splitting our resources, Frank. I'll keep Leanne with me. If he really means business, he'll also have Charlene by now. You must stay there with John, do you hear?"

"Of course," replied Frank. "Ray, be careful. This Noble character is either very brave or incredibly stupid. Whichever it is, it makes him dangerous. Good luck."

"Yes, and you too," replied Quinn. "I'll be in touch."

"Damn," said Quinn. "I didn't see that one coming. Drink up, we're off."

The accelerator of the BMW stayed pressed hard to the floor for the few minutes it took to get back to Priory Place. It was still in darkness, save for the lights on the driveway. Quinn bolted from the car and hammered on the front door. He was surprised to find it unlocked, but was grateful nevertheless. He sprinted the short distance to Charlene's room and was hugely relieved to see her looking up at him with an inquisitive frown. He saw that she had not yet got ready for bed. He breathed out heavily, and held out his arms to her. She came to him and they remained in a mutually enriching hug for what seemed an eternity. He was fast becoming a father figure to a vulnerable young woman who was very much out of her depth.

"Come on," he whispered, "let's get out of here."

Charlene allowed him to guide her to the car and slid onto the back seat. Quinn noticed that Leanne had moved into the back to be with Charlene and was pleased when she took her hand. He smiled his gratitude; at last she was thinking.

They drove in silence as Quinn's mind worked overtime. He did not return to the flat. If Noble wanted them divided it was better to let him believe he had succeeded. He would have to rely on Frank to look after John Lomax. He returned to the seedy run-down building that rented rooms by the hour. The nosy neighbour appeared right on cue, as if by magic.

"Hello again," she called. "We didn't expect to see you this quickly."

"What do you mean?" asked Quinn.

"Well, we saw the young man go in there," she said, "and he looked upset."

"Which young man would that be?" Quinn asked, his patience being tested.

"The same one as before. The one who went in with the brunette with hardly any skirt and tons of make up. Here, what's going on? That brunette never came out, did she? Is she still in there? Is that why the young man came back? I don't know what's going on, but it's all very fishy to me. I don't know what the world's coming to." She was building up a fine head of steam and looked to be heading for a long rant. Quinn didn't have the time.

"Thank you," he cut in, "you've been most helpful."

"You said that last time," she recalled, and her ample bosom expanded as she took in a huge gulp of air, ready to begin again.

"Yes, I know," Quinn continued, "and I meant it. Now, will you do me a favour? Keep a careful eye out and write down details of anyone who comes and goes from here. You know, dates, times, what they look like, what they're wearing, who they're with. Anything at all, in fact. You'd be doing me a huge favour. Don't tell anybody; it'll be our secret. I'll come back in a few days and see what you've got."

"How can I get hold of you?" she asked, swelling with pride at being asked to do such important civic duty.

"You can't," said Quinn, "as I said, I'll be back in a few days and call on you. In the meantime, don't say anything to anybody, not even the police. This is bigger than the local lot, and I've got to make sure security is maintained." He had adopted an imposing, official manner and the woman positively squirmed with delight at being the chosen one.

"You can rely on me," she affirmed with due seriousness.

"I'm sure I can," purred Quinn. "Now, excuse me, I must get on."

"Of course," she whispered.

Ray Quinn turned on his heel and strode into the building, aware of the woman's gaze on his back. Once out of her sight, he slowed to a halt. There was nobody around. He did not intend going anywhere; he was just killing time. He wanted Leanne and Charlene to wait long enough to believe he had been doing something. If he took enough time, he knew he'd be able to tell them anything when he returned to the car and they would believe him. They would have no reason for doubt. Although he didn't intend to go anywhere in the building, he couldn't resist stepping into the room in which Charlene had been incarcerated. The same room that Billy had been in with the brunette, she of hardly any skirt and tons of make up. The same room that Quinn had entered and dealt with the Harley jacketed man. The clean up team had been thorough. There was no trace of anything at all. The room was pristine. Actually, that wasn't true; the room was in a condition befitting the building in which it was located. It was ready for the next hour's rental.

"Bad news, I'm afraid," Quinn reported as he got back into the car. "It's obvious Billy's been here. There's some blood on the floor and a smear on the wall. I'm afraid something nasty has happened. He's obviously hurt, unless the blood belongs to somebody else, but I doubt that. You'd better be prepared not to see him again."

Ray Quinn looked into the back of the car to assess their reactions to the harshness of his delivery. Leanne looked away from Charlene and gazed out of the window, whilst Charlene took a sharp intake of breath and began to sob. He had been deliberately short and sharp. He was testing them both.

He allowed them an extended silence. Charlene was the first to find her voice.

"When? How?" she whispered.

"Recently, obviously," he replied. "I'm not sure of the circumstances just yet. I need to talk to Frank before we jump to any conclusions. If our not so resting man has taken Billy to Jack Noble, then he's in for a very uncomfortable time. He's tough though, isn't he Leanne?"

Quinn was referring to the episode in which Leanne had subjected her own son to some extremely nasty treatment in the not too distant past. Leanne's eyes widened in a plea for Quinn to go no further. He took pity and changed the subject for Charlene's sake, not for that of Leanne.

"We're going to have to follow the trail, wherever it takes us, ladies. Notice I said 'we.'

"It's not that simple," Leanne said. "I must be with John. He needs me more than ever now."

Whilst Quinn thought the sentiment admirable, he saw it for what it was. Leanne was petrified. She was unsure that she could cope with it all. She didn't want to be seen as weak, but knew she was. In her short sentence, Quinn could hear the desperate desire for her life to be normal, as it had been before the whole terrible nightmare had shockingly disrupted it, a need to step out of this surreal sequence of events. She hadn't yet recognised and admitted her part in it either. It was a common enough feeling for anyone following traumatic blows, and one with which he was all too familiar.

-25-

Ray Quinn selected The City Post because it boasted a huge circulation for a local newspaper. It focussed on the sensational and didn't pay much attention to the accuracy of its content. It reflected the approach of its editor, Ken Harvey, so he was also selected. It was living proof that sensation sells and it was housed in one of the city's newest and most impressive buildings. One of the triumphs of the building was the complete lack of parking space, so Quinn was forced to resort to using a taxi. He hoped he would meet his favourite cabbie again, but that wasn't to be. Once inside a vast open-plan lobby, Quinn hardly merited a glance from a whole bank of receptionists.

'I'd like to have a word with Ken Harvey,' he said, having selected one of the faces.

He was directed to a glass-sided lift, which would transport him up to the eighteenth floor, a ride that afforded a spectacular panoramic view over the city's sprawling urban skyline. It gave him a yearning for wide open spaces. It was a longing that had been growing within him for quite some time, and he knew it would lead to the heart of Exmoor, hopefully on a permanent basis. He had become disillusioned with city living, with its noise, dirt and dreadful anonymity. He had already promised himself and, more importantly, his wife that they would make the most significant move of their lives as soon as the current affair had been settled.

Ken Harvey greeted him at the door to his office. Despite the smoking ban in offices, and almost everywhere else, he still managed to carry the signs and smells of his addiction to tobacco. The effects of his forty-a-day habit, along with burning the midnight oil to meet ever tightening deadlines, were imprinted in his coarse complexion. Add to the picture his several chins and lank, thinning hair, and he did not present a physically attractive role model.

Quinn declined the offer of tea, coffee or mineral water on the grounds that they would all taste the same and thus best avoided..

Ken Harvey smiled and said, "I don't blame you. What can I do for you?" he asked as he squeezed himself behind an enormous mahogany desk, which was as scarred by life's battles as its owner.

"I'd like to talk to you about Jack Noble," said Ray Quinn.

Sizing up Quinn, Harvey broke into a broad nicotine-stained grin. "Oh yes. What's he done now?"

"He's running a vendetta at the moment," answered Quinn, "and he seems to have kidnapped a friend of mine."

That took the wind out of Harvey's sails. In fact, judging from the blanching effect on his face, it had scuttled the whole boat.

"Jesus Christ," he wheezed, "are you sure?"

Quinn nodded. "That's certainly how it looks."

"Jesus Christ," Harvey repeated. "I knew things were going on, but I didn't know the details."

"You must know him pretty well then." Quinn was alert now.

"We aren't what you'd call friends. I've run stories about him in the past, but I'd be wary now. He's not a man to be trifled with." Ken Harvey was also alert. "My pet theory is that he wants to become a national figure. He's already got most of this city in his pocket. I have heard, though, that there is somebody at the moment who is challenging him."

Quinn smiled at the newspaperman.

"Jesus Christ," he completed the hat trick. "You're either very brave or very stupid."

"I can assure you, Mr Harvey, I am certainly not stupid. Ask around," said Ray Quinn as he treated the man on the other side of the desk to one of his significant looks. "How would you like to have the sole rights to this story?"

Ken Harvey's baser instincts kicked in immediately. He saw the opportunity of national, as well as local, stardom.

"I'm not sure I follow," he lied.

"I intend to make sure my friend is recovered in rude health and this Jack Noble understands the error of his ways."

Ken Harvey was incredulous. "How on earth do you imagine you are going to do that?"

"Oh, that's simple. Your paper is going to report that my friend, his name is Billy Lane by the way, has been kidnapped and killed and the word on the street is that a local drug baron is involved." Quinn detailed his plan in matter of fact terms.

Ken Harvey was dumbfounded.

"Why should I do that?" he asked in amazement.

"Because you don't have a choice." Said Ray Quinn, smiling innocently.

"I think you need to explain yourself before I have you thrown out!" Harvey exploded. "You wander into my office without so much as a by your leave and tell me what I must do! I don't even know you. I've never seen you before. Who the hell do you think you are?" he was puce by the end of his outburst and breathless enough to have to sit down quickly.

"Please, Mr Harvey, take care. I've no wish to upset you. I'm here to give you a story the like of which you've only ever dreamed of. You'll be able to retire a rich man. Let me explain while you gather yourself. A few years ago a company called Anvex was robbed of well over £300,000. Although that's not a huge sum nowadays, it was worth more then. The thieves were never caught. You do remember it?"

"Of course I do," wheezed Harvey. "It led to a senior copper's death didn't it. DCI Sandy Lane, as I recall."

The penny dropped.

"This friend of yours, Billy Lane, wouldn't happen to be related, would he?" asked Harvey.

"Yes, he's DCI Lane's son."

"Wasn't there also something about a Leanne Lane as well," asked Harvey, becoming interested in where this was leading.

"Right again," said Quinn. What a fine memory you have. She was convicted of the copper's murder and ended up in prison. She's out now, of course, but I expect you also knew that."

"I remember," Harvey confirmed, "but what has this got to do with Jack Noble?"

"Patience my friend." The next part of the story laid out by Ray Quinn was a total lie, but the aim was to hook the newspaperman. "What you don't know is that there were two other people involved in the Anvex raid. They have fallen out since. One of them was Jack Noble. I represent the interests of the other. Jack Noble stole the proceeds from my client to set himself up in the drug business. He has now kidnapped Billy Lane as well. He also tried to kill my client with a drug overdose. My client wants to, how shall I put it?....rectify the situation. Oh, by the way, the police are not interested in any of this. They just want it cleaned up. They have promised to allow me to do just that. Between you and I, if certain people happen to fall by the wayside during my intervention, and that unfortunately could now include your good self, the blindest of blind eyes will be turned. I shall present you with the complete story, with full and binding permission to publish in your newspaper or even a book should you wish. Your part will simply be to publish exactly what I tell you at exactly the time I choose. It's a shame you now know all this. It means you are now part of the story, so you cannot refuse my offer. Your choice is between the chance any editor only ever dreams about, along with the income that will bring, and refusal. Actually, refusal is not really an option, because you know too much. Both my client and Mr Noble would agree on that point, and they aren't in agreement about much at the moment."

"I'm still worried. I need to check up on a few things." Ken Harvey was thinking about Jack Noble. He had contacts in that direction.

"Feel free, Mr Harvey." Quinn's confidence told Ken Harvey all he needed to know, so he began to set out what he knew about Noble.

"You will probably find him behind all sorts of things in this city, from the low level to the far more serious," Harvey ventured. "He has a talent for being involved in nefarious activity. Once he starts something he doesn't let it go. He is known to be persuasive, if you follow my drift, and is very good at getting people to go along with him. He is normally in a hurry to get results, but he has been known to bide his time. In other words, Mr Quinn, he knows how to get what he wants."

"He's sounds a formidable foe," offered Quinn.

"Exactly," replied Harvey, "I wouldn't want to cross him or be in his debt. Rumour has it that he hates being owed money more than anything else. Local legend has it that there are several bodies buried in concrete, holding up new buildings and motorway bridges."

"Nice man," commented Quinn. "Has there been any indication lately that things are getting too much for him?"

It took Harvey several seconds to meet Quinn's eye.

"The man thinks he's a pro. He views his work as others treat their careers.

"Has he any particular friends?" asked Quinn.

"I'm not sure that he has any what you'd call close friends. He gets along with anybody who serves the purpose of the day. In truth, he's a loner, and a dangerous one at that."

"Does he have a woman in his life?" Quinn pursued.

Harvey shook his head. "I never got the impression that there is anyone, but I suppose there could be."

"Do you know a girl called Sally?" asked Quinn.

"No, can't say I do." Harvey's reply was tellingly quick and Quinn spotted it.

"I know where I can find Jack Noble whenever I need," said Quinn, "but I've always found a little research never does any harm."

"Where is all this coming from? Where is it going?" Harvey was now more than worried. He fidgeted, played with his pen and couldn't hold Quinn's steady, probing gaze.

"Do I frighten you?" asked Quinn.

"No, of course not," Harvey replied. "I admit you've unsettled me, but scare me? No. Jack Noble frightens me, though."

"Let me give you a piece of advice, Mr Harvey. You've got it the wrong way round. You need to re-assess your perception. The status quo is changing around here and you'd be well advised to take notice and change accordingly."

The interview had run its course. "Well, thanks for your time Mr Harvey."

"No problem. Anything I can do," said Ken Harvey."

Quinn stood up but he saw that something was bothering Harvey.

"We can run this as a story?" he asked.

"It's news, isn't it?" said Quinn, drily.

"So what can we print?" Harvey was brightening now.

"Let's go for novelty. How about the facts?"

His sarcasm went unremarked.

"Which are?" asked Harvey.

"That Billy Lane was discovered dead late last night. Police are not currently looking for anyone else in connection with his death, but would like to speak to a woman who may have been at the scene, and a man who made the emergency call. Between you and I, Ken, I can call you Ken, I presume, I'm certain Noble is involved and I will make sure he will meet his maker, but you'd better not print that last bit, eh?" Quinn was at his sinister best.

"I'm sorry about Billy," said Harvey, making a valiant attempt at complete sincerity.

Quinn was impressed; a press man with a conscience was a new phenomenon. He thought about what he had learned. Although he had never personally dealt with the man on a one to one basis, Jack Noble was the name you heard everywhere around the city and it was always connected with just about anything criminal you could shake a stick at. Drugs, gambling, prostitution, Noble was up to his neck in it. Life was becoming rather interesting.

If Harvey printed what he'd been told, Jack Noble would either read it or know about it. It may even get to him from Harvey personally before being published. Quinn didn't care how it got to him as long as it did. He also knew Jack Noble would find out the origin of the story. He would surely find that the story came from Ray Quinn, which was what Quinn intended. He was flushing him out. He was intrigued as to how long it would take. The speed would be a measure of the man in his surroundings. A measure of his support or, equally likely, the fear he engendered.

-26-

Ray Quinn was tired of being in the field. When in the forces, especially when on operations, life had an edge; adrenalin coursed through his veins. The London 7/7 bombings had changed his life completely. John Lomax had saved his life and they had become firm and steadfast friends. He viewed life through different eyes. He had been retired on medical grounds and now his life had a changed meaning. He loved the freedom of the open road and his powerful bike. He did what he wanted whenever he wanted, with no exceptions. The first was his obligation to his saviour, John Lomax. He viewed it as a lifelong commitment and would walk to the ends of the earth for him. The second was his wife. Without her, he was nothing; his life would not be worth living. Now, he was at a crossroads. He needed to rid John Lomax of the spectre of Jack Noble and then withdraw to the quiet contentment of a settled retirement. His wife deserved it. She never pushed, but he knew it was time and he longed to be back with her now. She was patiently waiting for him.

Eschewing the inflated prices charged for the exotic beverages of the Chain Locker, Quinn deferred having a drink until he was closer to the flat. Being the centre of attention was becoming wearisome, but some ten minutes later he pulled into the car park of the Oak Tree Inn. His vehicle brought the total number to five, mainly because most of the Oak Tree's regulars were beyond the age when it was safe for them to drive. Lacking the dubious attractions of piped disco music, slot machines or wide-screen satellite TV, the pub was on borrowed time, ripe to be snapped up by one of the larger brewery chains and turned into one of the 'fun pubs' that, in Quinn's view, were too much of an assault on the senses to be anything like fun. He had heard it called an old man's pub, and not as a compliment.

He had been deliberately frequenting the pub on a nightly basis and Jack Noble would certainly know of his whereabouts by now. The only sounds to greet his ears in the Oak Tree were the clatter of dominoes that underpinned the low buzz from four elderly gents playing fives-and one at the end of the lounge bar. He went to the bar and ordered a pint of Guinness.

"I'll leave the car," he told the barmaid.

"Right you are, darlin."

It was something Quinn had been doing regularly; using the car as bait. In fact it meant he was also putting himself out there as he walked the 100 or so yards back to the flat. The others at the flat knew of his attempt to lure Noble to him and were worried. He had made Frank their guardian and nobody dared to challenge the arrangement.

His pint didn't last long.

The rain had stopped and, though it was mild for February, a fresh breeze blew as Quinn wound his way along the sixties-built cul-de-sac that was to the one side of the pub, and into the small service road that few people even knew existed. Ominously, a silver Ford Focus was parked just down from the flat. There was movement within, but no light.

His routine continued for several evenings. On each walk home, the silver Ford Focus was in the same place, as if it had not moved at all during the day. Quinn knew it had because the ground underneath it was wet. Nevertheless, it's vigil continued. The untrained eye would not have seen the movement inside its dark interior, but Quinn was very far from untrained. He spotted the dark shape that sat in the back seat and pretended not to look at him.

On the fifth evening the silver Ford Focus was in its usual place. Quinn knew something was odd. The car's interior light was on. Quinn's interest was piqued. He carefully checked his periphery, and then did a 360 degree circle rapidly, but he caught nothing. Not even a slinking cat.

Staying in as much darkness as possible he worked his way to the near side rear door of the car by the kerbside and peered inside. There, laid on the back seat was a prone figure. Quinn recognised him instantly. His training took over and he backed away carefully. He had seen too many of his comrades blown apart in dusty foreign places by just such a ruse. He inspected his surroundings again, but could see nobody. He knew he had to find out.

Inch by painstaking inch he crawled his way, laid out flat, using his elbows and toes to propel himself, until he drew level with the rear door. He knew he must open it, and that would be the time of greatest danger. With a last intake of breath, he pulled himself up and eased the door open. It was not locked. He did not open it fully. Bitter experience had taught him to open it as slowly and marginally as possible. It required a steady hand and an extraordinary courage. He had both.

He expected a wire that would trip an explosion if he opened the door too far, but there was none. He found out why. He was meant to find the body in one piece. As he moved it gently, its right forearm was exposed, with a needle hanging from a vein. It was a trademark that told Quinn everything.

Billy Lane's demise was faithfully reported in the City Post the next day.

'A body was discovered late last night. It is believed to be that of Billy Lane, son of the late DCI Sandy Lane and escaped murderess Leanne Lane. Police are not currently looking for anyone else in connection with his death as a self inflicted drug overdose is suspected, but would like to speak to a woman who may have been at the scene, and a man who made the emergency call. Our editor is personally taking charge of the reporting of this story and will have more tomorrow on Billy Lane and his life history.'

Ray Quinn reflected that Ken Harvey had gone beyond the brief he had been given and he would need to talk to him about that. He was also reminded of a line from a Kenny Rogers song, 'The Gambler.'

'The best that you can hope for is to die in your sleep.'

He promised himself, and Billy, that Jack Noble would not be afforded that luxury.

The flat was deep in shock that night and everybody went to bed much later than usual, almost as if sleep would bring unimaginable horrors. Leanne was inconsolable and John Lomax was bereft, but had to show stoicism for her. Charlene's reaction was unexpected. The only sentiment she expressed was a burning desire to go home to Australia and then she simply locked herself in her room. She was shutting out the world, lest it harm her any more. Frank took the opportunity of Quinn's presence to get some much needed sleep.

After everybody had gone to bed Quinn sat on his own a while longer with the window wide open despite the drizzle and the lights turned out. He breathed in the cool air and listened to the low, distant rumble of the city, punctuated incongruously by the occasional croon of nocturnal wood pigeons. The chirping of the phone jolted him back to the here and now and he scrambled to get it. He picked up the phone.

"Ray, it's me." said the voice from the other end.

'Me' was an old friend of Quinn's, who had steadily risen through the ranks of his macabre profession and was now a pathologist. Technically, he was not supposed to be talking to Ray Quinn, as an outsider, but Quinn was calling in favours from every direction.

"You're working late," commented Quinn.

"I know," replied the pathologist, "but all hell's broken loose here. Suddenly, all sorts of high up busy bodies have come out of the woodwork and want answers yesterday. Why must you cause such a stir wherever you go?"

"It's a gift," said Quinn, smiling to himself. "What have you got?"

"I've just finished writing up the notes on Billy Lane," he said. "I thought you might like a preview of the main findings. We've turned up some interesting stuff."

Upstairs, everything had gone quiet and Quinn said, "let's have it then," and listened intently as his friend gave him much more than mere preliminary findings.

"We were right about the drugs of course,' he said. "Billy definitely died from a massive overdose of diamorphine - heroin to you and me - but he did not administer it himself. Billy was right handed, wasn't he?"

"Yes he was," confirmed Quinn.

"But he'd injected into his right arm. Not normally a most natural thing for a right hander to do," went on the pathologist.

"Well nigh impossible, I'd have thought," said Quinn.

"So somebody did it for him," the medical man went on. "That's the implication, and Billy wasn't exactly co-operative about it. There's indication that he was forcefully restrained at the time he died. Extensive bruising to the wrists and upper arms, consistent with being held down. Along with some old and bruises whose provenance was unclear. We've run some basic forensic tests on the syringe, too. Significantly, there were no fingerprints on it, not even Billy's, meaning that whoever injected him either wore gloves or deliberately wiped it clean afterwards. It's not something suicides generally do." He finished.

"You'd know more about that than me," commented Quinn.

"The other curious thing is that the heroin used was of a particularly pure grade, although we're not sure how important that is at this stage. And the preliminary analysis of the blood that was on Billy's shirt shows that although it's consistent with the timing, the blood isn't his. We have to conclude that it was Billy's killer. Or one of them," the pathologist said.

"As you say," Quinn commented, when the monologue was complete, "interesting stuff. I can't thank you enough."

"Is my debt paid?" asked the pathologist, only half joking.

"Don't worry, I won't trouble you again," responded Quinn, "unless you find me staring up at you one day."

"God forbid," laughed the man at the other end, "I get nightmares enough without that happening. You'll make old bones, don't you worry. You're too careful and scary not to."

"Flattery will get you everywhere," replied Quinn, still laughing as he disconnected the call.

He had not noticed Leanne slip into the room, followed by Charlene. The first he knew of their presence was when Leanne switched on the lights. Leanne hung back to allow Charlene, who seemed totally withdrawn into her own world, to set her own tempo. Gradually reassured that it was safe, she began to pace, touching the walls and surfaces, checking them over. A plant pot smashed loudly to the ground, but Charlene ignored it. Leanne followed her at a distance. Eventually, having completed her tactile circuit of the room, Charlene gravitated to the TV, which she switched on without hesitation and, using the remote control almost instinctively, channel-hopped until she found something she liked, loud and brash with canned laughter. Choosing a corner of the room, she lay down on the polished wood floor, her knees raised and both hands in front of her face, peering through her fingers at the shadow cast on the ceiling by the standard lamp.

Her performance worried both Ray Quinn and Leanne, but neither spoke. Leanne stood watching for a moment, waiting for Charlene to get up again but she didn't. She did not understand what was happening, but knew instinctively that it wasn't good.

Ray Quinn also watched, mesmerised, but he understood perfectly. Shock does strange things and manifests itself in all manner of odd ways. He should know. He'd seen enough of it after the bombings as well as in theatre in the middle east. His experience told him to watch and not disturb; to wait for the victim to seek help.

John Lomax had also moved into the room quietly and, having slipped his arm around Leanne's waist, he stood watching a tortured soul in torment. He knew enough not to speak, so nodded to Quinn.

Eventually, Charlene rose from her position on the floor and retraced her steps in exact detail, finishing her performance tucked deeply under her duvet. She was in such deep shock that she would recall nothing of the night at all.

It felt like only minutes after closing her eyes that a crash startled Leanne awake, and she looked up to see Charlene flash by her bedroom door. Naked? Naked. In the bedroom her underwear lay on the floor in a soggy heap and there was a funny unidentifiable smell. She'd wet the bed. Ripping off the sheets, Leanne bundled them into a heap and took them into the kitchen, stuffing them furiously into the washing machine. The TV blared out from the living room but Leanne tracked Charlene to the bathroom where she was busily working her way along her row of toiletries, sniffing at each container of moisturiser, shampoo and talcum powder before pouring its contents into a congealed sticky mess on the floor.

"Charlene!" Leanne struggled to hold back her anger. Charlene just ignored her and kept on emptying. Her fury erupted.

"Stop!" she yelled.

Charlene stopped what she was doing and calmly walked over to her. She took Leanne's hand and pulled it towards the shower. Leanne thought she was asking, so she turned on the shower and tried to persuade her under the jet of water. Charlene wouldn't go, so she ran a bath and Charlene slipped into the water. She lay there happily, so happily that twenty minutes later when the water was tepid, she wouldn't get out. Help was needed, but there wasn't another female in the flat. In desperation Leanne grabbed the TV remote control and, dangling it in front of her as bait, pulled out the plug. It gurgled loudly and Charlene leapt out of the bath, snatching the remote and running through to the lounge, still dripping wet. Leanne gathered up what remained wearable of Charlene's collection of clothes. She dried her and then started to dress her. Charlene had other ideas and Leanne found herself physically manipulating her into every garment while she sat with his eyes glued to the TV screen. By the time Charlene was dressed Leanne was exhausted and they both looked as if they'd spent a night on the streets.

The commotion disturbed the rest of the occupants of the flat, and, no doubt, many neighbours as well. Nobody came to assist Leanne, however, and she felt completely helpless. She knew Charlene needed help, but did not understand what steps to take. She resorted to staying in the living room with her charge, whilst they both watched the TV.

Leanne had an idea. She would call the doctor. Charlene obviously needed medical help.

'I'm sorry," declared the irritatingly cheery reply, "there is no one here to take your call, if you would like to leave......" Leanne slammed down the phone in frustration.

She returned to Charlene and sat beside her once again, waiting for the rest of the flat to rouse themselves and rescue her.

Eventually, after what to Leanne seemed an eternity, first John Lomax and then Frank emerged. Ray Quinn was a little later. He was normally an early riser, having formed the habit earlier in his life, but nobody begrudged him the extra half an hour he had taken.

"Good morning, one and all," he chirped as he entered the kitchen. "I smell coffee; any for me?"

Lomax poured him a cup. Quinn took his time taking the first careful sips of the hot liquid, looking around his assembled troops through the curling, rising steam. He knew they were waiting for him to announce the day's activities. Eventually, just before he judged one of them was about to speak, he began.

"I heard the commotion last night. Is Charlene ok, Leanne?"

Leanne noted that he had spoken as if Charlene wasn't there. Perhaps he knew she had shut everything out.

"It's ok now," Leanne replied, "but it needs sorting out. We can't go on like this. Charlene needs proper medical help and counselling as well. I can't cope with her, especially straight after Billy..." she burst into tears and sobbed loudly. Lomax put his arm around her again.

"I agree," said Quinn. "We must get Charlene some help, and then we can concentrate on everything else."

"What do you suggest?" John Lomax asked.

"I've been thinking," replied Quinn. "Charlene's been to Priory Place before, but we had to get her out. But the picture is different now. I don't trust the doctor there, but at least he's a known quantity. If we get Charlene to go back there and leave Frank there as her guardian, there's no way the doctor can harm her. It would leave the rest of us to get on with what we have to do."

"How can you be sure she'll be safe?" asked Leanne, showing concern for a fellow member of the sisterhood.

"Because I would trust Frank with my life," he answered. "Believe me, there's nobody else to touch him. He scares me at times."

"That's good enough for me," put in Lomax, who was trying to distance himself from any responsibility for Charlene. He had been thinking overnight and come to the conclusion that she was not his kith and kin and was not even related by blood to Leanne, so why should he take any responsibility for her? All he wanted to do was to sort out this Jack Noble business and then settle into a quiet life with Leanne. It was a shame about Billy, but he had been weak too many times. Charlene's present state was Billy's fault completely.

Leanne had been listening intently, despite her sobs, and had come to a decision.

"I can't put her back in there," she pronounced. "It would be the end of her."

"What's the problem," persisted Lomax, "look at her; she's not exactly flourishing is she? Besides, Frank will be with her, and if Ray trusts him as much as he says he does, then she couldn't be in safer hands."

Leanne shivered as Lomax watched her efforts to come to terms with the situation.

"It's funny,' she said eventually, but went no further. Her eyes glazed over as she momentarily drifted off into her own thoughts, and Quinn could only guess at the images crowding her head. It was the stuff of nightmares. He began to wonder if she could cope, but in a matter of minutes she seemed to come round again.

"So what happens now?" she asked at last. She obviously assumed that her decision was binding upon them all.

"That's easy," replied Quinn. "I think we all need a break. We'll have a night out together. A few drinks, something to eat and some laughs. I know just the place."

-27-

Ray Quinn arranged a table at the pub for stand-up night. He remembered the last time he was there and knew it would serve his purpose. He had told them it was a night out; a break, to release pressure. He also said it may be just what Charlene needed. He had a private discussion with Frank to let him know the true purpose of the exercise.

"What do you think?" Quinn asked Frank.

"That you're a devious bastard. Remind me to stay on your side."

The Biker laughed with his friend. They shook hands as Frank set out from the flat to play his part.

"OK, ladies and gentlemen, let's go. We'll take a taxi. Frank's had to go out for a few minutes and has got the car. He'll join us there later."

Frank watched from a distance as they piled into Quinn's favourite taxi and rattled into the distance. He then drove the car back to the flat and left it there. He took another taxi and headed for the City Post offices.

Ray Quinn, John Lomax, Leanne Lane and Charlene sat at their table with drinks in front of them. Lomax noticed six chairs, but didn't comment. Perhaps Frank had gone to fetch someone else to join them. He didn't realise how right he was.

The familiar screech of feedback assailed their ears as the landlord took to the tiny stage at the front of the bar. There was a packed crowd as usual. Word had spread about the stand up nights.

"Where's your old lady?" came a cry from the back. "she still checking you've got the right size condoms?"

"Nah," shouted another wag, "they don't make 'em that tiny!"

"Now settle down, please, ladies and gentlemen. Let's have the usual warm welcome for out old favourite Annie Hall."

The crowd burst into applause as their favourite act levered herself up to the stage. She gripped the microphone in a very unfeminine fist and squeezed hard.

"Ohh, makes your eyes water. Glad she's not my old lady!" the crowd were in fine form.

"Now, now boys. Settle down, let's have some decorum," she instructed as her full face make up began to give the unequal struggle under the lights.

"I went to my golf club the other day," she began.

"Did you score?" came a cry.

"Nobody's that stupid," came a loud shout from the back.

"As I was saying before I was so rudely interrupted," she grinned through sticky bright red lipstick, a reporter was creeping to the pro yesterday. You're amazing, he said. You really know your way round the course. What's your secret? Easy, the pro replied the holes are numbered."

The crowd groaned in unison. It was reminiscent of old time music hall, and obviously very popular, as more and more people squeezed into the bar.

Annie Hall ploughed on.

"I remember when my old man and me got married. He had his golf clubs and all his kit with him at the church. I asked him what he'd got it for. He said, well this ain't going to take all day is it?"

"I would have 'it 'im with one of 'em," advised an inebriated voice from the crowd.

"I did," said Annie, quick as a flash. "He was a bloody mess. The police asked 'ow many times I'd 'it 'im. I said put me down for a five."

"Now 'ere's one for the gents. There are four most important things that you must 'ave in a wife. A pint for anyone who gets any of 'em."

The landlord shouted his agreement and the crowd cheered loudly.

"Any offers, then?" Annie called.

"She' as to be a good cook," came a call from the front.

"A pint for that man," yelled Annie and the crowd applauded,

"She ' as to make you laugh," offered another wag.

"A pint for that man," yelled Annie and the crowd roared its agreement.

"You 'ave to be able to trust 'er," another man shouted.

"A pint for that man," yelled Annie, giving away the landlord's profits with impunity and thoroughly enjoying it.

"She's got to be good in bed," and the crowd roared its loudest approval.

"A pint for that man," yelled Annie.

"Actually," she said, "there is another most important rule.

"We give up," bayed the crowd.

"You must make sure that the first four women never meet each other!" Annie landed the punchline.

"A pint for Annie!" screamed the crowd.

The mayhem continued around them and the group gradually relaxed and began to smile and eventually laugh. Quinn's constant supply of drinks helped eased the situation as well. Annie Hall finished her stint and departed to huge and raucous approval and the landlord announced a short break for people to replenish their glasses. He had to make up for the free drinks he had given away, after all.

"I wonder what's keeping Frank," said Leanne.

"He'll be here before long," promised Quinn.

-28-

Frank Quinn's taxi dropped him outside the City Post's magnificent building. It was way past normal working time, but various lights burned in random offices on several floors. Receptionists had been replaced by a single security guard in the entrance foyer. Frank waited for him to be occupied by a visitor and slipped past the lifts to reach the stairs. He pressed the lift button on his way past as a distraction.

Ken Harvey was not in his office and had his back to the stairs when Frank saw him. He only became aware of Frank's presence when he felt the prick of a sharp knife under his chin.

"It would not be advisable to move, my friend," said Frank, understating Harvey's predicament. "This is very sharp and my hand is not steady." The second part was a lie.

Ken Harvey froze.

"Who are you? What do you want?"

"All in good time," answered Frank. "You and I need a little chat. We should leave now, so walk calmly in front of me and be very careful; you've only got eight pints in your body, so you can't afford to lose much."

He walked the ashen and shaking Ken Harvey out of the building via the fire exit.

"Where are we going?" asked the newspaperman.

"I want to show you something," replied Frank, and he walked his man all the way to a certain drain, covered by a metal grill. "'Lift it up." He commanded.

Harvey bent down and strained to remove the object. He succeeded and stood up.

"No, stay there," ordered Frank. "Tell me what you see."

Harvey stared into the black abyss as others had done before him, and just like the others before him he was very afraid.

"Anticipation is a powerful force, don't you think?" asked Frank. "Can you see anybody down there? Perhaps if I turned you upside down it would help."

He swept Harvey's legs from under him and in one swift and dextrous movement had his opponent hanging over the drain, held only by his ankles. Harvey's bladder gave up the fight.

"Oh dear, it's lucky you're over a drain. Now, Mr Harvey, you made an agreement with a friend of mine about what you would print in your rag. What was it exactly? Word for word, if you please."

"That Billy Lane was discovered dead late last night. Police are not currently looking for anyone else in connection with his death, but would like to speak to a woman who may have been at the scene, and a man who made the emergency call", whispered Harvey.

"You are very fortunate that is exactly the correct answer. Now please tell me what exactly you did print? Word for word again, if you please.

"A body was discovered late last night. It is believed to be that of Billy Lane, son of the late DCI Sandy Lane and escaped murderess Leanne Lane. Police are not currently looking for anyone else in connection with his death as a self inflicted drug overdose is suspected, but would like to speak to a woman who may have been at the scene, and a man who made the emergency call. Our editor is personally taking charge of the reporting of this story and will have more tomorrow on Billy Lane and his life history." Harvey was in severe danger of his bowels copying his bladder.

"Well done, Mr Harvey. What an excellent memory you have. Now, my arms are getting tired and I may not be able to hold you much longer. I'm afraid it's happened before. Not very professional, eh? I really must get round to doing more weight training. I don't know whether they've found him yet. Obviously not, or your paper would have known, eh?"

Harvey wriggled in desperation.

"Settle down, Mr Harvey, please. Now, let's make an agreement you WILL keep. I have written down what your paper will print tomorrow. No ifs or buts. I'll put you down now, beside the drain and you will phone it through. Word for word, if you please."

He eased Harvey onto the ground and knelt over him as the call was made. Harvey turned over and was sick into the drain.

Frank leaned over so that he was whispering into the man's ear.

"Thank you, Mr Harvey, you've been most helpful. I'm sure the entire community will be grateful. I know Mr Quinn will also be almost satisfied. I don't think Mr Noble will be pleased with your latest literary effort, though. You are in a most difficult situation. On one hand you have an unhappy Jack Noble and on the other you have an unhappy Ray Quinn. A rock and a hard place if ever I saw one. I know which way I would choose, but, hey, I'm not in your position am I?"

Ken Harvey's eyes closed in abject fear as he heard Frank's words. They bulged open again as he disappeared into the black hole and was engulfed by the rushing foul black water.

Frank calmly replaced the drain cover and stood up.

"Most unfortunate," he said to himself, "just as we were beginning o get along."

He brushed himself down and strolled to the pub to join the others. No cabbie to give evidence later. As he entered he caught Quinn's eye, and shrugged his shoulders with his palms outwards in he age old gesture.

"Welcome stranger," mocked Ray Quinn. Won't you join us? There's a pint there on the table for you."

Frank noted that there was only one pint, but two chairs.

"Is your friend not coming along?" asked Quinn, with an innocent look.

"I'm afraid he had a prior engagement," answered Frank." He's had to pop along to interview some bigwig from the water company. He did ask me to give you this, though Ray. He said it would be on he front page tomorrow."

He passed Quinn the statement that was due to be published the next morning. Quinn scanned it and smiled his quiet smile. Jack Noble would not be pleased, he mused, which made him smile all he more.

Quinn suggested the group return to the flat as he had some news. When they were all sitting comfortably he read the statement.

"The City Post's front page tomorrow will carry the following in bold print.

"A body was discovered late last night. It is believed to be that of Billy Lane, son of the late DCI Sandy Lane and Leanne Lane. Police wish to speak to well known local businessman Jack Noble (pictured) in order to eliminate him from their enquiries. The public is warned not to approach him. Readers are asked to contact the police if they see him."

Quinn looked at each of his group in turn. He paid particular attention to Charlene.

"That's it. From now on, it's up to us. I will catch up with him, I promise, and he will pay."

Both Frank and John Lomax drew breath as one. They, more than anybody, knew what such a Ray Quinn promise meant.

"I suggest we all turn in for the night. It's been an eventful day and I think tomorrow will be even more, how shall I put it, interesting," said Quinn in a tone that nobody challenged.

-29-

By eleven o'clock, most of them had taken themselves to bed for the night, but Quinn remained in the living room going back over the details of the situation again and again, trying to find something, anything, that would prove a link to Jack Noble.

Frank appeared in the doorway.

"Bugger off," said Quinn, only half joking. "I'm trying to think."

Frank ignored him. "You might want to hear this," he said. "The women's refuge just phoned. They've had a woman show up there in a bit of a state. They don't think she's on booze or drugs, but the description fits Charlene. I asked them to keep her there. Here's a strange thing though. Those places don't normally allow men on the premises, but when I gave them your name their attitude changed. They said you could go in provided you brought a woman with you."

"It's a long story Frank, and I can't tell you about it because I swore to the people concerned that I wouldn't. You know how it is; if you need to keep a secret, don't tell another living soul. I'll have to go and Leanne will have to come with me. You stay here in case anything else comes up."

Quinn swept from the room and banged loudly on John and Leanne's door. "Leanne, I need you. I need you now. Stop whatever you're doing and hurry up. We have to go out."

Quinn was in a rush and had no time for niceties. Leanne poked her head round the door and looked at him questioningly.

"You choose your moments, don't you?" she said.

"Never mind about that," he barked. Get dressed and come with me. You've got one minute and no more."

She rushed from the bedroom five seconds after her deadline.

"Now, what on earth is so important?" she demanded.

"I'll tell you on the way," said Quinn as he pushed her out of the door and towards the car. "Get in; come on, hurry up."

He started the engine and began to move almost before she had settled into her seat.

"The women's refuge has phoned. They think they may have Charlene down there. I need a woman with me or they won't let me in. You've been elected."

"Does the fact that I'm the only female around have anything to do with it?" she asked tartly.

"I like your company," responded Quinn, meaning exactly the opposite.

He made sure he didn't attract any unwanted attention from roaming police vehicles, but still drove very quickly. They arrived at the refuge and Leanne pressed the intercom.

"Ray Quinn and Leanne Lane to see the manageress," she announced, putting her lips close to the microphone set into the wall.

There was a buzz and the heavily reinforced door, having decided to let them in, opened slowly. Waiting at the desk in the entrance hall with the manageress was a loudly protesting Charlene. She was filthy and her clothes stank, but Quinn wanted to hug her.

He walked straight up to her and, placing a firm, comforting hand on each shoulder looked directly into her eyes. He made sure she was looking at him before saying, "Billy is exhausted, so we left him asleep. He's Ok though. I had to bring Leanne with me because the people here insist on a woman being with you."

Leanne's lower lip trembled at the dishevelled and desperate state of the mother of her grandchild. "Hi Charlene," was all she could manage.

Quinn could see she was holding back tears. "She needs a doctor," he said.

"If you can wait a few minutes, we can get our on call GP to give her the once over," the manageress offered.

"No," Leanne said with unnecessary rudeness. "Her own doctor will do that. Come on, Charlene, let's go."

The manageress watched them leave the refuge and was puzzled by Leanne's curtness. She was, however, pleased with the outcome. There would be one less troubled woman in her care that night. She put her hands in her pockets, ready to prepare for the long night ahead. Her right hand found something and she rushed to the door in pursuit of the leavers. Ray Quinn turned round at the sound of her approach and took a couple of steps towards her. It was enough to take him out of the earshot of the others.

"I almost forgot," said the manageress," I found this in Charlene's coat pocket."

She handed him a mobile phone. He closed his hand round it and touched her fingers at the same time. She couldn't help herself as she self-consciously blushed.

"Thank you," he said, pressing her hand in return. "I mean thank you for what you've done for her," he said. I'm glad it was you who called."

"No problem, she replied. "I'm glad it was you who came. It's good to see you again. Sorry about having to bring a woman, but it would have looked very strange if we had ignored the usual protocol."

"I understand," he replied. "Keep in touch."

"I will," she whispered as he turned to take his leave.

"You make an impression wherever you go," said Leanne acidly.

"It's a gift," he replied, "or a curse. It depends."

Leanne chose not to pursue the topic.

"You said we've got our own GP," said Quinn. "Who do you have n mind?"

"Well," she offered, "I thought that doctor at Priory Place seemed ympathetic and helpful, but I think we should clean her up first."

Charlene and Leanne fell asleep in the back of the car even nough it was a short journey and they had to be woken when Quinn topped outside the flat. Charlene was so groggy that she didn't ven protest when Leanne put her under the shower, and afterwards he munched her way slowly through almost a whole pizza while eanne put a call through to the doctor. Inevitably, all she got was ne after- hours answering service, but moments later the doctor imself called her back. With some difficulty, Leanne explained what ad happened. The doctor was typically unfazed and full of ympathy.

"And how are you," he asked solicitously.

Leanne was struck by the thought that when a patient enters a doctor's surgery she is often greeted with the words "how are you today?" She had always thought that a stupid question because if the patient was well, she would have no need to attend the surgery in the first place. She had often been tempted to reply "I'm well, but thought I'd drop in and ask about you." It would be far better for the doctor to ask "what can I do for you today?" In fact, she mused that would be a good name for a doctor's quiz team. She was somewhat taken aback by his kindness, but was pleased as well.

She restricted herself to "Fine thank you. A little tired, but nothing too bad. It's Charlene I'm called about. We've just been called to pick her up from the women's refuge and she's a mess. We wondered if you'd take a look at her."

"Bring her to Priory Place and I'll meet you there," he replied. "I'll let them know you're on your way."

"I appreciate that," said Leanne, thank you."

She put the phone down and looked at Quinn, who had heard everything. She knew she had been pretty unpleasant to him and her anxiety about Billy and Charlene had compounded the feeling, but he didn't really deserve to be treated badly. After all he done for Lomax and the rest of them, she felt very guilty about her own responses to him. She must apologise and resolved to do it later when Charlene was settled.

"Frank will take you," instructed Quinn. "I have something I must attend to here."

Leanne wondered whether he was stepping back to give her time with Charlene. She also thought he may be giving her the space to formulate a proper apology. In fact his reason was much more down to earth. He had been thinking of the encounter with the manageress at the refuge. She had been trying to tell him something without using the words and he needed to find out what it was. He had a feeling, a gut feeling, that he was being told something about Leanne. He always trusted his gut feelings and he saw no reason to change its tried and tested success rate.

Quinn took Frank aside into the kitchen. "I think it would be a good idea if you let Leanne take the lead with this," Quinn said to Frank. "It might be better coming from a woman, and besides, I want you to take careful note of her throughout. There's something wrong here. We'll talk when you get back."

"No problems," replied Frank. He knew that when Ray Quinn had instincts about something he was invariably correct.

"Is everything ok here?"

"Fine."

Leanne sat in the back with Charlene on the way to Priory Place. Nothing was said at all, but the silence was comfortable. They were let in almost immediately after Frank had pressed the buzzer by the doctor in person.

"So, how's the patient?"

"Ok, we think," she replied, "but very quiet. Silent in fact."

"Do you recognise the doctor?" asked Leanne.

Charlene had already seen who it was and was suddenly animated again. In fact Frank saw sheer abject terror on her face.

"No! No! No! No!" she shouted, backing away from the doctor hastily.

Leanne was stunned. Charlene was obviously more traumatised than she'd realised.

"Charlene! It's all right. It's Dr Boyle, Charlene. He's your friend." She tried to reassure her, casting the doctor an apologetic smile. "I told you. She's all over the place." After a few minutes, she managed to calm Charlene by fetching her a drink.

Dr Boyle dismissed Charlene's reaction with his customary understanding. "She's been through a lot. It's not at all surprising that she should be reminded of the ordeal. It might help if I prescribe you something to help her sleep, just for a few nights, until she's back into normal routine again."

Sitting down at a table in the hallway, he took out his prescription pad and pen and scribbled down something. "Now, let's go and have a look at her." This time Charlene remained passive while Leanne helped the doctor listen to her chest.

Leanne's mobile buzzed into life. "I'll take it in the hallway," she said, to minimise disruption. It was Ray Quinn.

"Hello, how's it going?" he enquired.

"All right, thanks." Now that he was on the line, Leanne didn't know quite what to say to him. "Look, I wanted to.." but as she spoke something caught her eye. Something embossed in gold on the leather case of Dr Boyle's prescription pad: JAN, the capital letters all interlinked. That was interesting. Leanne's mind raced, as she grappled to achieve some kind of coherency to the invading thoughts.

"Are you all right, Leanne?" Quinn asked from the other end of the line.

"Yes," Leanne said, immediately distracted by further unease in her brain. Why was the doctor so helpful, so solicitous? He was only a duty doctor after all. Granted he was attached to Priory Place, but it was above and beyond the call of duty to come out here at night at such short notice, wasn't it? Why had Charlene reacted so strongly when she saw him? Leanne shivered violently as understanding took shape.

"I've got to go," she said suddenly. "The doctor is examining Charlene."

"Okay," said Quinn, uncertainly. "We'll keep in touch."

She could sense his confusion at the other end of the line but she had to give herself time to think this through. There would be a reasonable, rational explanation for everything. All she had to do was ask.

"Dr Boyle," Leanne walked back into the lounge, but unexpectedly the doctor and Charlene weren't there. She went through to the bathroom. "Charlene, Dr Boyle," she called out, bewildered. She returned to the examination room and, finding it empty, she rushed back out into the hallway. What the hell was happening? Then she noticed that the door to the stairwell was slightly ajar. She was lucky to have seen it, because it normally banged closed as it was pulled shut by its spring. Struggling to quell a rising panic, Leanne rushed through the closing door and sprinted up the stairs, her fears beginning to crystalise. This late at night everything was deathly quiet and there was no one around. Her blood ran cold.

"No," she gasped out loud. Charlene!"

Leanne burst through the front door onto the roof to see Charlene and Dr Boyle standing by the waist height railings, like a couple of old friends admiring the view. The doctor turned towards her.

"Leanne," he said, mildly, stretching out a beckoning hand, "why don't you join us?"

Leanne walked slowly towards them.

"What's going on? What are you doing?" she asked, hoarsely, her voice barely audible even to her own ears as she struggled to regain her breathing.

"Surely you must have already worked that out, Leanne, "the doctor smiled. "I'm protecting myself. I have to make sure that no one will ever know."

She was chilled to the marrow. Her misgivings were right.

"I can help you," she said, realising how feeble it sounded.

-30-

As weird phone calls went, that one was off the scale, thought Quinn. Leanne hadn't completed her sentence when she was interrupted by something. He had the feeling she was about to apologise for something, but couldn't. Then there was the manageress at the refuge. She had definitely been trying to tell him something. Perhaps he was wrong. Perhaps his gut instinct had let him down for the first time or were these disparate and seemingly unlinked pieces of a jigsaw coming together? The last few days had been a hell of a strain on them all. He was exhausted. He couldn't do this anymore. He needed a drink and to sleep for a very long time.

His mobile prevented any of that.

"Frank?" said Quinn.

"Get here now!" barked Frank.

He knew his ally well enough. Grabbing his helmet, forgoing his leathers, Ray Quinn roared into the black night.

At the same time the doctor was talking to Leanne.

"I don't want your help. I only want to square my account with John Lomax. It's unfortunate that you're here, but I can't get to him except through you. In fact, to hell with it; all of you deserve what's coming. You're all the same."

In the white glow cast by the floodlights his face took on the grotesque appearance of a gargoyle.

"'What can you hope to do?" Leanne said, finding sudden strength. "I'm not here alone, you know that. The man with me won't let you get away with it and Ray Quinn's on his way. You know what he can do, don't you? If anything happens to us I would not want to be in your shoes."

The doctor smiled grotesquely. "It will be an accident. They'll understand. It's the kind of thing that could have occurred at any time, especially now, when Charlene is so traumatised."

"What accident? What are you talking about?"

But even as she spoke, Leanne knew.

"How far would you go, Leanne? How far would you really go for Charlene? Or John Lomax? Or the little boy? Charlene's not blood is she, Leanne? Billy was but she'll get the little boy, so you won't see much of your grandchild anyway. The child needs his mother. You need to make the sacrifice for his sake. That would be a noble thing, Leanne, wouldn't it?" he coaxed her by using her name over and over again, as he took a step nearer to the edge.

Ray Quinn's mind was racing at a speed that was equal to his bike.

'Christ, I can't believe I didn't see it before. It's been there all the time, staring us right in the face!' The streets were steady with traffic even at this time in the evening, but with enough slack for the machine to make rapid progress. He dreaded what he would find. "Please God, let me not be too late," he murmured under his breath.

He roared into the drive and sprayed gravel and grit everywhere as he slammed on the brakes. His eyes searched for clues. He forced himself to rely on his training, his experience. He saw the BMW and noticed the car beside it.

"And there it is," he said to himself.

There was even a 'Doctor on call' sign resting audaciously on the dashboard.

"On the roof, Ray," called Frank, but Quinn only partially heard him as he ran.

"Don't let anyone out of this building until I say you can," Quinn shouted back over his shoulder.

He used the run up the stairs as thinking time. It had been quite a while since he had experienced any action such as this and he orced himself to think clearly. The doctor's car was the clue. He had seen it before, but where?

The roof garden was beautiful. An effort had been made to create a soothing green oasis away from the stress of city living. But in the ight of the horror unfolding before her it had become monstrous and ugly. Leanne was exhausted and part of her just wanted this over. She wanted to close her eyes and for this to end. But she had to keep Dr Boyle talking. If he let go of Charlene now, it would be disastrous. But she needn't have worried. The last couple of days had reaped one advantage at least, and Charlene was clinging to he doctor like a leech.

The doctor was still cajoling, coaxing. "Believe me, I don't want to hurt you or Charlene. It's Lomax I want. He owes me money and nobody gets away with that. I can't get to him, so it has to be like this."

He was sickening. Leanne couldn't imagine now how she'd even iked the man. Beads of sweat had broken out on the doctor's upper ip. Leanne was close enough now to see them glistening in the light.

"How many have died?" she asked. "How many have died at your hands? You may not have killed them yourself, but the drugs you put on the streets did. You're sick! No, you're repulsive."

Charlene moaned and wriggled at his side.

"She's getting bored," he said. "We should get this over with."

Leanne wouldn't let it go. Why should she make it easy for him?

"It's simple," she heard him say. "It's your decision. Charlene or you? I'm going, but who with?"

"How do I know that you won't let Charlene fall anyway? Why should I trust anything you say?"

"That's your choice, of course. But you're her only chance, Leanne." The doctor relinquished his grasp slightly and Charlene struggled to wrench herself free.

"Wait!" Leanne blurted, desperately. "I'll do it. You don't have to hurt her. She won't give you away. Look, I'll do it."

Feeling suddenly weightless with fear, her legs shaking almost uncontrollably, Leanne stepped up on to the first and then second rung of the railings. The doctor watched, urging her on with his eyes. She glanced below to where the city streets swayed and blurred. So this was how her life would end, in ultimate, futile sacrifice.

"Leanne, stop!" Another voice rang out over the roof and with overwhelming relief she recognised it as Quinn's. "You don't have to,' he said. "It's over. Walk away from the edge, doctor, and bring Charlene with you."

Everyone on the rooftop froze.

"It's the only sensible thing, doctor," Quinn continued, ersuasively. "You can't win this. We know what you've done. We've ust heard your confession. You have nothing to gain by this now. here's nowhere else to go."

For what seemed an eternity nothing happened as the doctor esitated, weighing up his situation. Leanne halted, poised on the recipice. Seconds ticked by, everything deathly silent, but for the ackground hum of an ignorant city amplified by the light rain that ad begun to fall. Then miraculously the doctor began, inch by inch, ɔ move back across the roof towards Ray Quinn. For a moment it ɔoked as if he would comply, until suddenly, as Leanne's foot ɔuched back down on the roof, he shoved Charlene to one side, ɹrned and lunged for the railings.

Frank had disobeyed his friend's instructions and was by now lso on the roof. Quinn yelled at him to stay put as Charlene, anicked by the sudden activity started running towards the outer dge of the roof.

"No! Leanne screamed. Quinn took a flying leap at Charlene, ringing them both crashing heavily onto the concrete, but for the octor it was too late. Frank, trained by Ray Quinn in the forces, obeyed the command instantly and without question. He watched with detachment as the doctor hurled himself over the edge to certain death.

Retaining a tight hold on Charlene's clothes, Quinn got to his feet and walked over to where Leanne stood, dazed and shaking. By the time he reached her, Frank had put a protective arm around her.

"Come on," suggested Quinn, "let's get off here."

The men shielded the women's eyes as they skirted around the mutilated body of the doctor. Frank loaded his precious human cargo into the BMW whilst Quinn prepared to mount his bike. They returned to the flat in convoy. When they arrived John Lomax was there to hug and kiss his loved one and Charlene. He had ordered yet another Chinese takeaway and it didn't last long even though nobody professed to being hungry. It was the shared experience of a communal meal that was important.

"What made you come back tonight?' Leanne asked. "Was it my phone call?"

Quinn was tired and sore. "Don't flatter yourself," he answered. "Your call certainly got me wondering. But when we picked Charlene up from the refuge, the manageress gave me a mobile phone she found in her clothing. I traced the calls on it. One of the names that featured on it regularly was a Dr Boyle. Two plus two make four.

"Not bad for a beginner. Thanks for showing up," she said, unable to prevent sarcasm spilling out.

Quinn put a hand to his heart and mocked her. "Ouch," he said.

"I was trying to say I'm sorry, I've been a bitch."

"Well, the last few days haven't been much fun, for you have they? Although I must say, I've enjoyed myself. But if you want to make it up to me you could spend the rest of your days keeping out of trouble and looking after John. I want a quiet life from now on and I want to spend time with my wife." Quinn announced.

Leanne smiled her agreement, but couldn't stop herself from making one last comment.

"That shirt's a mistake by the way, she said, grinning from ear to ear. "I'm not sure that the bloodstain effect really works."

Quinn glanced down at where blood had seeped through the fabric. "My wife's going to love that," he said, "but she knows I've no eye for fashion."

The following morning their final arrangements were settled. Lomax and Quinn had already had a long discussion which resulted in the arrangements that were now outlined to everybody. John

Lomax and Leanne returned home to run the jewellery shop, the business buoyed by a substantial boost. Charlene, her small son and her parents were put on a cruise ship at Southampton to take the slow route back to Australia. There was no way she could face being trapped in a flying tube. Her bank account had been injected with sufficient funds to open a jewellery shop, as part of the growing family empire. The business partnership would ensure they all got together as regularly as possible, but not enough to fall out. Nobody dare argue with any of it. The last detail was that Frank agreed to take over Quinn's role as protector of one and all. He knew he would be kept busy for the foreseeable future.

They stood together in the living room before Quinn was due to leave. He was already dressed in his full leather biking gear and held his helmet in his left hand. There was a prolonged silence as each didn't know quite what to say.

"I'm curious," John Lomax eventually broke the embarrassment, "we've got all this money, we've split it up and you don't seem bothered about Jack Noble. In fact you've not mentioned him since we got back last night. How can we be sure it's all over?"

"Where do I start?" teased Quinn. Firstly, the prescription pad bore the initials JAN. They stand for John Anthony Noble.

Secondly, the other car at Priory Place had a 'doctor on call' notice in the windscreen. Two and two make four. Finally, I knew he was Jack Noble anyway."

"But how? Lomax asked.

"That's none of your business," replied Ray Quinn enigmatically, as he turned and strode out through the door. They had shaken hands firmly earlier and their mutual friendship had been recognised. It would remain unchanged. He hated goodbyes, anyway.

Outside, the rain had turned into a steady downpour. Frank turned up his collar ineffectually against the torrent and walked into town to flag a taxi. He also hated goodbyes. Ray Quinn, still sore from his cuts and abrasions, sat astride his bike and gingerly coaxed it out into the traffic.

-31-

Ray Quinn drove with skill and care. He was enjoying the warming sun which was pouring though the car's panoramic window. His wife sat beside him and let the scenery unroll before her.

"Do you remember the last time we went to Exmoor?" she asked, looking across at her newly reclaimed husband.

"Of course, my love. It's gorgeous there," he replied, wondering what was coming next.

"I think I'm going to buy a horse and go for long rides," she said wistfully.

"Well don't expect me to come with you. Damn things are evil. I prefer to be in control of what I sit on, thank you very much. I'm not going anywhere near something that's got four legs, has a mind of its own, has sharp metal on the end of its legs and is that big. I'll stick to my bike. Oh, by the way, you did pack that copy of T.S Eliot didn't you? I'm going to become intellectual," he grinned.

"Of course I did."

Quinn hoped she would consider the subject closed and concentrated on driving the car.

Silence prevailed for many miles as the car carried the happy couple towards their new beginning.

"Raymond," she said, after a suitably long silence.

Quinn was immediately alert. She only ever used his full name when there was a problem. His mother used to do a similar thing just before telling him off. She never lost the habit, even when he had fully grown into adulthood. There's something about mothers, he thought.

"Raymond," she repeated, "this is all very nice and I know we are going to have a peaceful time living on Exmoor, but is this really the end of it all?"

"What do you mean," he asked warily.

"I mean what I said. Have you really retired? Is this the end of you solving the world's problems by yourself? Can you actually switch off now?" she continued.

"Which question would you like me to answer first?" he teased.

"Don't be obtuse," she replied rather sharply. "Have I got you all to myself from now on or not?"

Ray Quinn let silence fill the car again. The passing breeze was barely discernible and he caressed the steering wheel as he guided the car round a bend. A pheasant wandered across the road in front of him and seemed unconcerned by the possibility of imminent death.

"Stupid things, pheasants," said Quinn, pleased that he had avoided the meandering bird. He had also avoided giving his wife an answer and he knew she had noticed.

Lightning Source UK Ltd.
Milton Keynes UK
UKOW06f1711300316

271200UK00008B/342/P